A PERFECT HERO

"What sort of man did you think I was, that I would leave you in distress?" Spencer's blue eyes narrowed.

"I did not know you when we met at the earl's wedding," Elizabeth burst out. "I was desperate to accept your offer of help, as I had run out of options. And most men would be loath to interfere in another man's betrothal, no matter how irregular."

"I am not most men," he murmured, moving a step closer to her.

"That I have come to learn," she replied, transfixed by the indefinable expression in his eyes.

"In fact, I do find myself most willing to interfere in another man's betrothal," he said, continuing to regard her.

His focus on her began to make Elizabeth self-conscious. She had never in her life been assessed with such intensity, not even by the most formidable of business foes. And never in a business meeting had she been suffused with the warmth that seemed to seep from her chest to every extremity under Mr. Willoughby's gaze.

"You do?" she whispered inanely.

He did not answer her. Instead, he gently raised one bandaged hand to her face . . .

BOOK YOUR PLACE ON OUR WEBSITE AND MAKE THE READING CONNECTION!

We've created a customized website just for our very special readers, where you can get the inside scoop on everything that's going on with Zebra, Pinnacle and Kensington books.

When you come online, you'll have the exciting opportunity to:

- View covers of upcoming books
- Read sample chapters
- Learn about our future publishing schedule (listed by publication month *and author*)
- Find out when your favorite authors will be visiting a city near you
- Search for and order backlist books from our online catalog
- Check out author bios and background information
- Send e-mail to your favorite authors
- Meet the Kensington staff online
- Join us in weekly chats with authors, readers and other guests
- Get writing guidelines
- AND MUCH MORE!

**Visit our website at
http://www.kensingtonbooks.com**

MISS SCOTT MEETS HER MATCH

Laura Paquet

ZEBRA BOOKS
Kensington Publishing Corp.
http://www.kensingtonbooks.com

For Paul, with love and thanks.

ZEBRA BOOKS are published by

Kensington Publishing Corp.
850 Third Avenue
New York, NY 10022

All Kensington titles, imprints and distributed lines are available at special quantity discounts for bulk purchases for sales promotion, premiums, fund-raising, educational or institutional use.

Special book excerpts or customized printings can also be created to fit specific needs. For details, write or phone the office of the Kensington Special Sales Manager: Kensington Publishing Corp., 850 Third Avenue, New York, NY 10022. Attn. Special Sales Department. Phone: 1-800-221-2647.

Zebra and the Z logo Reg. U.S. Pat. & TM Off.

First Printing: September 2002
10 9 8 7 6 5 4 3 2 1

Printed in the United States of America

One

The elegant streets of Mayfair flashed by in a blur of gray stone and wrought-iron fences as Elizabeth Scott ran, and ran, and ran. She stumbled once on a loose cobblestone, and still she ran. She almost bowled into a young girl selling flowers, and still she ran.

"Miss Elizabeth! Please, Miss Elizabeth!" she heard her maid, Jenny, gasping.

She spun around to see the plump young girl panting and red-faced. And behind her, about three streets away, she glimpsed a too-familiar figure in a long black greatcoat.

"Jenny," Elizabeth hissed, "I'm so sorry I've involved you in this. But now I need you to do an errand for me."

"An errand, ma'am?"

"Yes." Elizabeth gripped the young girl's hand, squeezing it for emphasis. "Go now, quickly, down that lane. It should take you back to Oxford Street. Once you get there, find our carriage, and have Wallace drive you back home as quickly as he can." She paused, thinking quickly. "When you get back to the house, tell the butler to make sure that the doors are locked, and to ensure that the biggest footmen are ensconced by all the entrances."

Jenny nodded, her eyes wide.

"Then tell my aunts where you last saw me, and tell them that Victor is following me. Let them know I'll be home as soon as I can elude him. Beg them not to leave the house until I return. And please tell them not to worry." Elizabeth glanced past her maid again. Victor had cut the distance between them by almost a street. "Go, Jenny, please. Quickly!"

The little maid's lower lip quivered. She stayed planted in the middle of the pavement.

"Please, Jenny!"

"This don't feel right, Miss Elizabeth. Leaving you here alone. Wallace will skin me."

Elizabeth gritted her teeth. "I will be perfectly fine, Jenny. It is not as though I am a green girl out on the town. A spinster of three-and-twenty is of no interest to anyone. I do not fear for my reputation." That was the least of her worries at the moment. She glanced up the street. Victor was less than two streets away. "My aunts will be concerned about me. Please go set their minds at rest."

"Why don't you come too, Miss Elizabeth?"

"Because, Jenny," she said, trying to keep the frustration out of her voice, "Victor would just follow me home, and I would be right back where I started. I don't want him to find me."

Nibbling nervously on her lower lip, Jenny glanced across the street and seemed to come to a decision. "Be careful, Miss Elizabeth!" she cried as she darted into a break in the passing parade of gilded carriages and splendidly mounted riders.

Gasping with relief, Elizabeth wasted no time looking behind her yet again. Heedless of the annoyed glares of nearby pedestrians, she plunged forward along the pavement. She bolted into a side street, earning herself a shout from the dandified driver of a high-perch phaeton who had to rein in sharply to avoid her.

I'd rather be run down by a horse than by Victor, she thought as she scurried down the street lined with tall-windowed town houses. Several more pins escaped from her once-elegant chignon, sending unruly curls into her eyes.

At the end of the short thoroughfare, Elizabeth glanced behind her. Victor was nowhere to be seen, but she doubted that he had given up the chase. Blindly, she turned right into a narrow mews. Victor would keep going, down to the major street ahead. Would he not?

She couldn't take any chances. If her wretched cousin caught up with her, he could surely overpower her. And then it would not be long before they would be standing before two witnesses and an unscrupulous vicar, Elizabeth thought with a shudder.

The idea spurred her through the dingy mews on exhausted legs. Praying that it was not a cul-de-sac, she sprinted past a stable, ignoring the gaping visage of a clearly amazed groom. Her breath rasped in her throat, tore at her lungs.

A commotion behind her claimed her attention.

"Surely you could not miss seeing a young lady bolting like a racehorse!" she heard Victor's harsh voice echoing from the street she had left behind.

Desperately, she scanned the alley, but saw nothing but locked gates and closed stable doors. Then she spied a sturdy ladder leaning against a high stone wall. Judging by the branches of a plane tree she could see at its top, the wall probably enclosed a substantial garden. Looming behind the tree she could just see a range of chimneys. Like a drowning woman flailing for shore, she ran toward the wall.

"I did see a woman, sir, galloping as if the hounds of

hell were behind her," she heard a deep voice booming from the street.

She reached the ladder, placed one slippered foot on the bottom rung, and began to climb.

"I must say, Matt, you always do provide the most excellent punch," Spencer Willoughby said with a contented sigh as he raised a crystal goblet to his lips. "None of that insipid sugared water so many others offer as refreshment."

"Glad it meets with your approval." Matthew Carstairs, Earl of Langdon, grinned as he came down the steps from the house and crossed the deserted garden toward his old friend. "Finding it a bit hot indoors, were you?"

"Just slightly. It is quite the crush in there. Never knew you had so many friends."

"I do not, and well you know it. Half of them are political colleagues I have been cultivating, while the rest are part of Clarissa's rather extensive acquaintance. She is the social butterfly, not I."

"Suppose you will have to get used to such gatherings, now that you are leg-shackled."

"Suppose I will," the earl replied, his grin widening. "But since I have been 'leg-shackled,' as you so charmingly put it, for just over an hour, I hope you can forgive me if it is taking a little time to become accustomed to the idea."

"Accustomed to the idea of what?" came a gay voice from the terrace. Lady Clarissa Denham—no, the Countess of Langdon, Spencer reminded himself—sailed down the steps to stand beside her new husband. He slipped his hand around her waist and squeezed her tightly to his side.

"This social whirl into which you appear to have plunged me."

"It will do you the world of good to become more social," the new countess said, her eyes twinkling. "And if a man cannot be convivial at his own wedding breakfast, when can he be?"

"You are right, my dear," her husband conceded. "I am learning that she usually is," he added in a stage whisper to Spencer.

Spencer smiled and moved to lean against the stone garden wall as he watched his friends spar with each other. A year ago, he would never have believed the Earl of Langdon would make a love match. Hell, until a few months ago, it seemed unlikely that he would make any match at all, until he had met Lady Clarissa.

He was glad his friend had fallen in love with the vivacious young woman at his side, instead of contracting a loveless society marriage, as Langdon had initially desired. For one way or the other, the earl had needed to wed. Peers had obligations to perpetuate the line.

Automatically, Spencer thanked the powers that be that he had no such obligations. As the fourth son of a baron, he faced no expectations from anyone.

"You two certainly appear to be the happiest of couples," he remarked, raising his glass of ruby-colored punch. "To the bride and—"

Before he could finish his impromptu toast, a heavy object grazed his shoulder, knocking the glass from his hand. A plume of punch sailed through the air, coming down squarely in his eyes and momentarily blinding him.

"What the devil?" he cried, just as he heard a muffled moan from the grass beside him. Wiping the punch from his eyes with a corner of his formerly snowy neckcloth, he looked to the ground and saw, to his astonishment, a horror-stricken young woman with a magnificent mane of brown curls tumbling down her back.

"Oh my heavens, sir, I am so terribly, terribly sorry. I lost my footing on the wall, and I did not see you there. Look at your neckcloth, and your lovely jacket! They will be ruined!" Gasping, she struggled to her feet. "I shall pay to replace them."

Spencer wondered if he was addled from the heat and was having some sort of bizarre dream. "What on earth were you doing on the wall?"

"Running away from . . . well, just running away. I was racing down the alley, and then I climbed up the wall to escape. I had intended to look around before I jumped, but then my slipper caught on the hem of my dress and I lost my balance." She pushed a long curl from her eyes and stood face-to-face with him—well, almost face-to-face, as she was a head shorter than he. That was not so surprising. At about five feet, she would be shorter than almost everyone. "I am so dreadfully sorry. Are you injured?"

"Only my pride," he murmured, simultaneously stunned at her breathless recitation and captivated by her wide, intensely green eyes. "Since no one here knows us both, please allow me to introduce myself. Mr. Spencer Willoughby, ma'am." He gave a slight bow.

"I am Miss Elizabeth Scott, sir."

He knew not how long he might have stood staring into those eyes, if he had not suddenly become aware of a male throat being cleared. Jolted from his reverie, he turned to face Matthew and Clarissa.

"Miss Scott," he said, feeling a trifle absurd under the circumstances, "allow me to introduce my friends, the Earl of Langdon and his new bride, the Countess of Langdon."

"New bride?" asked Elizabeth as she curtsied, glancing at Clarissa's elegant blue silk gown. "Oh my goodness, have I interrupted your wedding?"

"Just the breakfast," said Clarissa. "Please do not be

concerned. You appear to be in a state of great emergency. Can you tell us from whom you are running? And why you are trying to escape?"

Elizabeth looked from one to the other, her expression suddenly hooded. Spencer deduced that she was hesitant to share her tale with strangers. Could she be a thief?

Possibly, he conceded. But the chances that someone so elegantly dressed was embroiled in a life of crime seemed highly unlikely. Besides, he was already loath to believe anything ill of her.

"I believe that, before we proceed further, we must conceal Miss Scott in some manner," he said. "Once she is safe from her pursuer, we can hear the whole story."

"A wise idea." Matthew tapped his chin. "She could easily blend into the crush inside. One more guest will not be noticed."

"Really, my lord, my lady, Mr. Willoughby, I must protest!" Elizabeth exclaimed. "You do not know me. For all you know, I could be here to steal things during your party."

There, Spencer thought. *If she was truly a thief, she would not have exposed her aims thus.*

"I have disrupted the festivities enough already," she continued. "Please, if I may just have a few minutes here in the garden to catch my breath, I shall be on my way."

"Nonsense." Spencer shook his head. "Your pursuer will not have given up so easily. He may still be lurking in the neighborhood, awaiting your reappearance." A thought struck him. "Is there anyone accompanying you? A maid, perhaps?"

"There was. I sent her home with word of my whereabouts."

"Then it is settled. You shall join the party as our honored guest." Clarissa laid a gentle hand on Elizabeth's arm. "Please, come inside. My maid can help you repair your hair and provide you with anything you may need."

"Thank you. You are too kind." With a backward glance at the two men, Elizabeth allowed Clarissa to lead her across the terrace and into the house.

"You may want to come inside as well, Spence. That neckcloth is ruined, but my valet may be able to save your waistcoat, if we act quickly."

"Hmm." Spence remained rooted to the ground, watching the passage of the two young women through the conservatory.

"Distracted, my friend?" A gentle smile creased Matthew's face.

With a guilty start, Spencer laughed. "Perhaps a little. She is a rather intriguing young woman. And who could possibly be pursuing her through the streets of Mayfair in the middle of the day? It is most odd."

"It is that. Although you look as though you might enjoy pursuing her yourself. You haven't made any conquests recently, now that I think on it." Matthew turned back toward the house. "I would say you're about due."

"Somehow, I suspect that Miss Scott would not prove as easy a conquest as the young actresses at Drury Lane."

"Perhaps you have just been using them to rehearse with." Matthew turned back to give his friend one last knowing look before going indoors.

Perhaps, Spencer thought. But actresses did not care much for a man's fortune or prospects, and they did not care much for marriage either. Spencer had an uneasy feeling that Miss Elizabeth Scott was made of sterner stuff.

Twenty minutes later, Spencer found himself in one corner of Stonecourt's massive drawing room, studying Miss Scott's profile as she chatted with Clarissa's younger sister, Lucy. And a fine profile it was, too.

Clarissa's maid had gathered the stranger's abundant brown curls back into a loose chignon, and had even found a few pearls to wind through her coiffeur. Now it was easier to see Miss Scott's pale complexion and pert snub nose. Suddenly, she laughed at something Lucy said, and a deep dimple sprang up in her cheek. Fascinated, Spencer crossed the room to stand at her side.

"I see you are somewhat recovered, Miss Scott," he murmured.

"Yes, quite, thank you, Mr. Willoughby."

"May I offer you ladies a glass of punch? You see, I seem to have spilled my own glass, and so I am in search of some myself."

"I am very sorry that you spilled your punch," Miss Scott said, blushing. "And yes, I should love a glass. And you, Lady Lucinda?"

Lucy smiled. "Thank you, but I must excuse myself. Clarissa and Matthew shall be leaving soon, and I need to speak with Clarissa before they depart."

"Then it shall be just the two of us, Miss Scott. Shall we proceed to the punch fountain?" he asked, holding out his arm to her. She placed her hand on his sleeve, and he felt a jolt of energy surge through his veins. Good Lord, there was something most captivating about her.

Could she be a skilful criminal, on the run from the authorities? Had she used her charming demeanor to commit some dreadful act? He could not make himself believe so. And yet, he needed to know the truth, and quickly.

Once they were settled on a low sofa in a relatively quiet corner of the morning room with glasses of punch, he turned to her. "Miss Scott, I hesitate to pry, but I wish to help you. From whom were you running? What do you fear?"

The smile that had played about her lips faded away and some of the color drained from her face. Glancing around, she said in a low voice, "I am running from my cousin. Well, in actual fact, he is my second cousin." She seemed about to say more, then stopped, twisting her hands together in her lap.

"Your cousin?" Spencer prompted her.

"Yes. Yes, he . . . he is trying to . . . to blackmail me." She took a deep breath, then spoke in a rush. "Or, failing that, to force me into marriage with him. But I will not marry him. I will not! He shall not win. He has brought all of his problems on himself, and he has no right to force them on me."

Spencer blinked in response to this extraordinary speech. "Your cousin is trying to blackmail you? How? With what information?"

She paused, then shook her head. "I do not wish to reveal that, sir. It is a nasty story about my family, one that is no fault of mine but that I truly do not wish to reveal to the world."

"It is no matter," said Spencer, turning over the matter in his mind. Despite her evasiveness, he trusted that she was telling the truth, as far as she dared tell it. Unless she was an extremely skilled liar, she was truly in distress. The question was, how could he help?

"The main thing we need to do now is to keep you safe from this man until we can find a way to solve the problem," he said. "Will you be safe if you go home?"

"Safe?" Miss Scott appeared puzzled by the question. "As safe as I am anywhere in London, I suppose. Except on Chapel Street," she added.

"Chapel Street?" he inquired.

"A small, rather deserted lane off Oxford Street. I was heading for a millinery shop there with my maid when he chased me down."

Spencer filed this bit of information away for later reference, but did not comment on it aloud. Instead, he tried to clarify his previous question. "What I meant to ask was whether you are secure at your home. Do you have family members living with you who can help protect you?"

At this question, she gave a small smile. "Unless you count my two aged aunts, I do not. And they are dears, but hardly the sort to engage in a pitched battle with Victor. We have several strong footmen, but most of our servants are somewhat elderly. And my parents and my brother are dead. I am the only one left, you see, and that is part of my problem."

Spencer, who did not see at all, seized on the issue at hand. "I do not think it wise, then, for you to return to your home. Surely, that is the first place your cousin will attempt to find you."

"But where else could I go? I have responsibilities, and I cannot simply disappear indefinitely."

"Not indefinitely," said Spencer, tapping his fingers against the back of the sofa. "Just until we can find a way to keep you safe. But . . ."

"Excuse me, Mr. Willoughby. You have been more than kind. But you are not responsible for my security. I have imposed too much already."

"Think nothing of it. It is not as though I have a great deal to occupy my days. Little is expected of me, so I have ample free time to do a good deed or two. And am I to let you return to your home, only to wonder whether you will be attacked or blackmailed the very next day? I may not be much more than a decorative fribble, but I do have a bit of a conscience." He smiled to temper the bitterness he could not seem to keep out of his voice these days.

Miss Scott did not reply immediately. Then, slowly, she raised those amazing emerald eyes.

"You do not seem a fribble, Mr. Willoughby. Do not talk so."

He chuckled, but did not reply. Just as the silence was becoming uncomfortable, his companion sighed.

"I truly do not wish to impose, but I must admit that I am at something of an impasse. I have tried everything with Victor. First, I attempted to reason with him. Then I offered him some money—not everything he demanded, but enough to satisfy any reasonable person. I have even considered legal action, but such things take more time than I had imagined." She frowned. "Perhaps, if I just had a few days of peace where I was not constantly on my guard to evade Victor, I could devise a solution."

"And I shall help," Spencer said. "I have the perfect place for you to hide. Do you enjoy the country, Miss Scott?"

"I have not had much opportunity to sample country life, as my responsibilities have long kept me tied to London. However, I once went to Sussex to visit a friend, and found my time there most rewarding." She paused, twisting a swath of her yellow silk gown into a tortured crease between her fingers. "But what did you have in mind?"

Spencer mentally berated himself for not proposing his idea more bluntly. Of course, she was hesitant to accept a virtual stranger's offer to bundle her off to some isolated estate.

"Please do not trouble yourself. It shall all be respectable, I assure you. I was about to suggest that you accompany my mother—and me—to Linden Park, our estate in Staffordshire. We have plans to go there tomorrow in any case. And this evening, you shall stay at my mother's house in Mayfair." He grinned, pleased with the simplicity of the plan. And, he had to admit, with the prospect of additional time in this mysterious lady's company.

"Will your mother not object?"

"My mother is the most sensible of creatures, and she cannot bear to see anyone in trouble without doing her utmost to help. I shall speak to her, but I am certain it shall not be a problem."

Miss Scott closed her eyes for an instant, then opened them and rubbed her hands together briskly. "Then I thank you, Mr. Willoughby. You are doing me an enormous favor. I must, however, send word of these plans to my aunts. They are likely already distressed about my absence."

"By all means. I shall ask one of Langdon's innumerable servants to direct you to a quiet corner and to supply you with paper and ink. One of his footmen can carry your note immediately to your aunts—by a circuitous route, in case he is followed. And I shall unearth my mother and introduce you."

With that, he strode away, into the crowd of revelers.

Elizabeth watched him cross the room, his blond hair like a beacon in the throng. He certainly cut a fine figure, even in this most elegant assembly. His dress coat of blue superfine was of the best cut and in the highest stare of fashion. And his buff pantaloons set off his calves to most excellent advantage. There was something about him—an indefinable flair—that set him apart from the men she normally encountered. But of course, they were from two different worlds. Was that what attracted her to him so?

She pulled herself up short. How could she be ruminating on the cut of Mr. Willoughby's coat and on his undeniable charm when there were so many more pressing matters at hand? The primary one being, of course, this scheme he had concocted. It did not seem rational to run away from one man into the protection of another. At least she knew Victor—knew what he wanted, and how he was likely to attempt to get it. She knew this slight blond aristocrat not at all. And suddenly, she had agreed to flee London with him, on simply his word that he would keep her safe. Had she lost her mind?

She had tried for many years to curb her impetuous tendencies—although, in times of stress, she still tended to take rash actions, such as climbing ladders and vaulting over walls into unknown gardens, she thought ruefully. But considered, logical decisions were vital to the success of the import business she had inherited from her father. Elizabeth prided herself on the ability she had fostered to "reason like a man." So why was she involved in this mad plan?

Because there was no other choice. Victor had shown he would stop at nothing, not even assault, not even kidnapping, to get her money. If she returned home, she would be a virtual prisoner. He would likely find a way to reach her even there, eventually. And he would not have her money. Not one penny.

"Are you all right, Miss Scott?" A concerned voice interrupted her musings. Elizabeth looked up to see young Lady Langdon hovering over her, a worried frown creasing her forehead.

Elizabeth forced herself to smile. "I am fine, my lady. You have been most welcoming to me, and on this of all days. I don't believe I have even given you my best wishes on your marriage."

Clarissa grinned. "Thank you. I am just so delighted today that I wish to share my good fortune with the world. The little we have done for you is nothing." She settled herself on the sofa.

Surveying her fashionable companion, who radiated happiness from every pore, Elizabeth felt a stab of something she rarely experienced: jealousy. She had never had much interest in marriage, having always been too caught up in managing her family's business. Vaguely, she had assumed that sometime, in the deep and distant future, she might find a man willing to countenance the thought of a wife whose interests lay more in the Royal Exchange and the wharves than in embroidery and household management.

But glimpsing the joy shining from Lady Langdon's eyes—this was obviously a love match—she wondered if, perhaps, she should have put more thought into the whole marriage endeavor.

I could always marry Victor, she thought with distaste. *But I'd rather fry in hot oil.*

She suddenly became aware that Lady Langdon had asked her a question. "I'm sorry. I'm afraid I was woolgathering."

"No matter. You have much on your mind. I was asking whether you had had a chance to meet Mr. Willoughby's mother. She is a most delightful woman."

"I have not yet, but he has left to find her now." Elizabeth paused, then rushed on. "I need to ask you something, quickly, before he returns. And please answer me truthfully."

"Yes?"

"What sort of a man is Mr. Willoughby? I know he is your friend, and so this question is most impertinent, but I must know. Can I trust him?"

Clarissa laughed. "Mr. Willoughby is the most trustworthy man I know—excepting Lord Langdon, of course! He and my husband have been friends since their days together at Oxford, and I know that Matthew trusts him implicitly. As do I. He is one of the reasons we are wed, you know."

"Really?"

"Yes. A plan he suggested to my husband gave us time to get to know each other properly."

Elizabeth chuckled. "He does seem to be quite the man for making plans. He has devised a plan to hide me, by spiriting me away to his parents' estate. His mother will accompany us. But I just wanted to make sure . . ."

"That he has no evil designs? I may be a biased source, but I can assure you that Spencer does not have a devious bone in his body. What he does have is a genius for finding just the solution to others' troubles. He always seems to be helping someone or other out of a tricky spot."

Elizabeth assessed the woman sitting next to her, much as she would assess a gentleman approaching her with a business proposition. She had trained herself to look for shifting eyes, perspiring foreheads, uneven breathing and other signs that all was not as it should be. But Lady Langdon gazed back at her with an open countenance. Perhaps too quickly, Elizabeth came to a decision.

"If you are certain he is above reproach, I shall accept your word," Elizabeth said. "Please forgive me for even asking."

"Do not think twice about it, Miss Scott. One can never be too careful, especially as a woman. But sincerely, do not trouble yourself about Mr. Willoughby. You are safe in his hands."

Elizabeth believed that in her heart. And as she sat on the sofa awaiting Mr. Willoughby's return, she silently willed her mind to agree. Much was riding on the success of their plan.

Two

"Of course, my dear, you must stay with us in the country, at Linden Park, for as long as it takes to get your affairs in order," Caroline Willoughby, Lady Riverton, said. "Your cousin shall never think to look for you there. Even if he saw you run down that alley, he will think you are with the Langdons. And they have disappeared on their honeymoon." Lady Riverton smiled, satisfied with their plan.

After the wedding breakfast had broken up, Elizabeth had accompanied the Rivertons to their London town house. Now, she gazed around their spacious first-floor drawing room, as she analyzed her current situation. All did appear to be in order. And yet the idea seemed too simple. Victor Newfield had shown himself to be a very determined man. She hesitated, trying to find the words to express her gratitude for the plan, as well as her doubts that it would work.

Mr. Willoughby spoke up. "And yet, we need to take additional precautions to protect Miss Scott. Her cousin, I suspect, will be desperate to find her. You said that his gambling debts had become ruinous, did you not?"

Elizabeth sighed. "Yes. My illustrious cousin has few skills, but one of them is incurring debt upon debt. He has an unquenchable weakness for any kind of wager: cards, horses, the weather, anything. That sort of thing may be fine for those who have nothing better to do"—

she felt herself blushing at her accidental implied criticism of the aristocracy, but she plunged ahead—"but Victor has managed to ruin his business as well. He has no other means of support. His creditors will soon cut him off, if they have not already done so. Although we have despised each other since we were children, I am his last chance to avoid scandal and debtors' prison."

She felt her face twist into a bitter grin. "Or, to be more precise, my money is his last chance."

"Forgive my rude inquisition, but we must know the facts of the situation to be able to protect you," Mr. Willoughby said, his kind blue eyes focused on her. "We are to assume that you are in possession of a sizeable fortune?"

"Yes." She paused, uncertain how much of her private affairs she was willing to reveal to virtual strangers, no matter how charming. Things that were general public knowledge among the traders of the Royal Exchange surely could not be dangerous, she decided.

"My father founded an import business. Its success lies largely in trade with the West Indies: cotton, coffee and sugar. I am now the sole owner of the company," she began.

"My dear, however did you learn to manage such a large business? It is highly unusual for a woman to be involved in such an occupation, particularly as the firm's proprietor." Lady Riverton's voice was not unkind. She was simply stating a fact that was no secret to Elizabeth. And her question was one Elizabeth had grown accustomed to answering since she had begun learning her father's business at the age of thirteen.

She had yet to learn how to answer it without a wave of sadness washing over her, however.

"My parents did not originally intend that I should be involved in the company at all," she murmured. "My older brother, Anthony, was to take over the firm. He started training with Father when he was fourteen. But two years later, he was killed in an accident."

As Lady Riverton and her son murmured their sympathy, Elizabeth took a deep breath. All these years later, she still found it hard to think about the day her father's clerk had brought Tony's lifeless body back from the busy wharves.

"Since I was the only remaining child, and had always shown an aptitude for geography and figures, my father decided that I should be taught the import business. He was obsessed with the idea that my future livelihood should be my own responsibility, not that of managers and servants. My mother opposed the idea initially, but then she saw how much it was helping my father cope with Tony's death. In a way, it helped all of us. We learned to look ahead, instead of behind."

Elizabeth reached toward a platter of cakes on the rosewood Sheraton table before her and selected a seed cake, placing it absently on a tiny plate. "And so I was brought into the business at the age of thirteen. It turned out to be a very prescient decision on my parents' part, as it meant I had the experience I needed to take over the day-to-day running of the company earlier this year." Again, she paused, gathering her thoughts.

"My father died of influenza in February," she said, her voice flat even to her own ears. "My mother caught it as well, and passed away in March."

"Oh, my dear . . . " Lady Riverton began. At the same time, Mr. Willoughby said, "How terrible, Miss Scott . . ."

Quickly, she continued her story before their well-meant concern made her weepy.

"I admit that the decision to bring me into the company was highly unconventional. But I enjoy the work, and I am glad that I have been able to maintain Father's legacy."

"He would indeed be proud of you," said Mr. Willoughby. Elizabeth could not tell, from his neutral voice, whether he found her success admirable or freakish. When he did not expand on his comment, she continued.

"I need depend on no man for my security, which is exactly what my father had hoped. He had not anticipated, however, that a man might come to see me as *his* security." Elizabeth sighed. "Unfortunately, Father made no provision to protect my money from fortune hunters. He could have placed my assets in a trust, but neither of us saw the need to do so. As a single woman, with my family's property legally willed to me, there was no question that everything I owned was mine to do with as I wished."

Elizabeth looked at the concerned faces that surrounded her. "I had assumed that, if I ever decided to marry, there would be ample time to set up a trust to protect at least some of my assets. At a minimum, I would need to ensure that I had status as a separate trader."

"What is that, Miss Scott?" Lady Riverton inquired with interest.

"It is a status for women available only in the City of London. As a separate trader, I would be permitted to continue my activities with my father's company. Without that status, I would be unable even to sign a contract."

Lady Riverton nodded. From the expression on her lovely face, it was clear that the idea of signing contracts on her own behalf had never entered her mind.

Elizabeth was familiar with the sensation of coming across a wholly new and previously unconsidered idea. "It had never occurred to me that I could be forced to marry against my will, without the opportunity beforehand to settle my affairs," she said, frowning. "I could kick myself for my laxity."

She picked up her delicate Wedgwood cup of tea before continuing. "Yesterday, I sent a note to my solicitor to arrange a meeting. I told him I intended to start proceedings to protect my funds, the business, and my property. Once that is done, I will be of no further interest to Victor. Until it is done, however, I have no doubt he will try everything in his power to find me."

"I think you are right in that assumption," said Mr. Willoughby, pushing himself away from the green marble mantelpiece against which he had leaned for most of the discussion. He began to pace in front of the glowing hearth. "But I do not believe it is safe for you to visit your solicitor here in Town, nor even to have him visit you here. Your cousin likely knows the identity of your solicitor, and may be watching his office."

"He does know that Mr. Lewis handles my affairs." Elizabeth squeezed her hand into a fist as she felt despair wash over her. Every time she thought she had found a solution to her problem, another complication arose to obstruct her.

"I propose that we ask our man of business to work with Mr. Lewis. Your cousin will not recognize him, and he can report back to you at Linden Park." Mr. Willoughby continued to pace.

"Do sit down, Spencer," his mother said. "You shall wear a hole in that carpet."

"I am sorry, Mother, but I think better on my feet." Bearing out the truth in his words, he strolled behind the silk-upholstered sofa where Elizabeth sat. She suppressed an urge to turn around and watch him, concentrating instead on his well-modulated voice as he continued to assess her situation. The faint aroma of sandalwood teased her senses.

"If you are to disappear to the country for a few weeks . . ."

"A few weeks!" Elizabeth set her teacup down on the Sheraton table with a clatter. "I cannot leave the business for more than a few days. And I cannot impose on your generosity for such a length of time." She began to rise to her feet.

Very briefly, she felt a hand on her shoulder—a warm and gentle touch that almost distracted her from Mr. Willoughby's next words. "Please, Miss Scott, hear me out. I know it is disturbing to leave your business for such a length of time, but having dealt with solicitors before, I know it will be neither quick nor simple to resolve your affairs in such a manner that your cousin will not be able to find a loophole with which to ensnare you."

Reluctantly, she sank back onto the sofa, but she did give in to the temptation to twist backward to look at him. His gaze rested—unseeingly, she suspected—on an indeterminate point on the yellow-striped wallpaper on the opposite side of the room.

"And, with you safely hidden at Linden Park, I shall have time to do a bit of investigation."

"Investigation?" Elizabeth said, loathing the note of panic she heard creeping into her voice. "What sort of investigation?"

"I want to find out more about Mr. Newfield. Anyone who would try to force his way into an innocent young woman's money to pay his own debts is obviously a coward. And cowards, in the end, can always be frightened. Anything I can learn about your cousin's affairs may come in useful when it comes time to tell him that we have thwarted his blackmail plans."

"That does seem like a logical plan," Elizabeth conceded, breathing an inward sign of relief that his "investigation" did not seem focused on other, more dangerous, channels. "Of course, I will tell you everything I have been able to learn, which I must admit is not much. Victor's associates, not surprisingly, do not seem all that willing to share information with me."

"So you agree that it is wise for you to disappear for a few weeks?"

Elizabeth sighed. "I suppose I do. You have made a most persuasive case."

"Good. I am glad my skills in that area have finally served me some more useful purpose than convincing the fine people at White's to put another bottle of claret on my account." He chuckled.

White's, Elizabeth noted. *So he spends a great deal of time in the clubs.*

"Now, to practical matters," Mr. Willoughby continued. "If you are to leave Town for an extended period, you must inform your aunts of your whereabouts."

"Goodness, my aunts! I cannot possibly leave them in Town alone." Elizabeth looked wildly about the room. "What on earth was I thinking? This chaotic day has addled my brains. Who knows what Victor might do to them in an attempt to draw me out?" She shook her head. "I thank you most kindly for your offer of sanctuary, but I must not leave London. My business is one thing, but my aunts' safety is quite another." She laid a hand on the armrest of the sofa.

"Miss Scott, please do not be hasty!" Mr. Willoughby spoke from behind her. "Your presence at your home will put your aunts in greater danger, as Victor will be tempted to try to capture you there."

She puffed out her breath in utter frustration. He was correct, of course. Was there no practical solution to this unspeakable situation with Victor?

Then an idea occurred to her.

"I know what I shall do!" she exclaimed. "I shall send a note to our warehouse, asking that several stevedores be assigned to our home as extra security. They are huge men, and Victor is at heart a coward. If he does not think I am in residence, he will not risk a fight with one of them." She grinned, pleased at her contribution to the plan, which all agreed made eminent sense.

"Then all is arranged," Lady Riverton said. "We shall leave as soon as possible in the morning."

Elizabeth hesitated, then drew a breath to speak. There was one more issue she simply had to resolve. "I should like to send for my manager, Gerald Reynolds," she announced.

"I know it is a risk to bring him here," she hurried to add, anticipating Mr. Willoughby's response. "But while I trust solicitors to talk among themselves about the legalities of my estate, I must speak directly to Mr. Reynolds. There are business issues we must discuss before I leave, and I must impress upon him the urgency of reassuring my aunts."

Behind her, Mr. Willoughby sighed. "I do not like it. He could be followed here."

"Oh Spencer, stop worrying. Honestly, you do fuss," his mother said.

Mr. Willoughby's voice was cool as he replied. "I am simply considering all the elements of the situation."

"As you do so well, dear," Lady Riverton said, and Elizabeth flinched at the subtle note of dismissal in the older woman's voice. She had heard a similar tone many times herself, in the midst of business negotiations with traders who clearly believed her incapable of handling commercial affairs.

"But I think you are being too mysterious about this," Mr. Willoughby's mother continued. "If you are so concerned, should we not consider bringing in the Bow Street Runners?"

Elizabeth gasped. "Oh no, Lady Riverton. I do not want to draw any attention to myself. Rumors can spread quickly—and rumors are often the beginning of the death of any business." And truths of the sort Victor could spread about were even worse than rumors.

"I understand completely," Lady Riverton assured her. "No one likes a scandal, however unjustly it is foisted upon one. But do you feel you can trust your manager? Is he a longtime employee?"

"He has been with the company since before I was born. In fact, he was my father's best friend, and he is my godfather."

"Then it is settled." Lady Riverton stood. "Send for him. Advise him to make his way here carefully, and all shall be well."

"No," Mr. Willoughby said, moving out from behind Elizabeth's sofa.

"Pardon me?" Elizabeth said, bristling. The idea appeared sound to her, and she was becoming weary of arguing.

"No," Mr. Willoughby repeated. "I do not believe Mr. Reynolds should come here. Again, he could be followed. I suggest that a meeting be arranged elsewhere. Perhaps my rooms in St. James's. As they are located in a building with many occupants, even someone watching Mr. Reynolds's movements would not be able to determine which resident he was calling upon."

"In St. James's!" Lady Riverton's voice was as sharp as broken glass. "Spencer, have you taken leave of your senses? Miss Scott can no more be seen on a street in St. James's than she could acquire a membership at White's. Her reputation would be ruined."

It would be ruined if she found herself married to Victor Newfield, as well. Before Elizabeth could voice this thought, Mr. Willoughby replied.

"Then she shall not be seen. We will arrive in a hired coach, and she can wear a mantle with a large hood. I believe I have seen several such garments in your wardrobe, have I not, Mother?"

"Yes, but—"

"She can easily slip into my rooms without detection.

I shall not be the first person, nor the last, to smuggle a lady into the august precincts of St. James's." His voice was laced with dry amusement.

Had he done it before? Elizabeth rather suspected that he had.

"That appears to be a logical plan to me," Elizabeth said. "Truly, Lady Riverton, do not worry about my reputation. Do not forget, I am used to appearing at the Royal Exchange and in other venues that females do not normally frequent."

Lady Riverton sighed. "If you are comfortable with this scheme, Miss Scott, then I suppose I should agree," she said, the mulish expression on her face suggesting that it was seldom she did not get her way in any sort of argument. "But I insist on accompanying you. To chaperone."

"Of course, Mother. I would not deny you this chance to glimpse my palatial surroundings." Spencer chuckled.

"Very well, then. It is settled." Lady Riverton rose from her chair.

"All is not settled yet, Mother," Mr. Willoughby said, beginning to pace. "How shall we explain Miss Scott's presence at Linden Park to the household staff and the neighbors? I do not think it wise to give her true identity."

"Really, Spencer, do you honestly think . . ." Lady Riverton began.

"No, my lady, I believe Mr. Willoughby is right," Elizabeth said. "Victor may be foolish when it comes to money and gambling, but he is by no means stupid, and he will be looking for me. I think it is wise not to use my own name."

Mr. Willoughby continued his restless progress around the room. "I think we should let it be known that Miss Scott is a distant relation of ours, as well."

A distant relation of the aristocracy. How ironic. "That is eminently sensible," was all Elizabeth said aloud.

"Elizabeth, you must be crazed! You cannot possibly leave London at this time!" Gerald Reynolds, a florid man whose flamboyant waistcoat gaped slightly over a rounded belly, had bounded up from his seat in Spencer's small but neat sitting room, nearly upsetting a glass of his finest port in the process.

Spencer was sorry enough he had wasted good wine on this bombastic man. It would be doubly unfortunate if the port ended up on the floor.

"I am not crazed, Gerald. Surely you can see that I must do what I can to keep out of Victor's sight until I can resolve my legal affairs. It is ultimately to the company's benefit, can you not see?" Spencer heard a quaver in Miss Scott's voice, but she held firm to his plan, as she had throughout her manager's tirade.

"All I can see is that you are abandoning us to our own devices, just weeks before the *Margaret Rose* is due to arrive from Kingston. We need you in the office, not haring off to points unknown!" The older man took a gasping breath, and shook his head. When he spoke again, his tone was wheedling. "The least you could do is tell me where you intend to spend your weeks in hiding. I am your manager, after all. Do you not trust me with that information?"

Miss Scott sighed. "We have discussed all this, Gerald. I will be staying with Mr. Willoughby's parents, Lord and Lady Riverton. To reach me with any urgent messages, simply deal with the Rivertons' man of business. He shall communicate with me immediately." She stood up, signaling the end of the interview. "The last thing I need is to have Victor badgering you, or my aunts, for information on my whereabouts. I know that is unlikely, as you two are barely passing acquaintances. But if he does approach you, all you need say is that you do not know. He will know quickly enough that you are telling the truth."

"And do you not fear that he shall try to beat it out of me?" Reynolds whined.

Despite Miss Scott's trust in her godfather, Spencer was running out of patience with the older man. He decided it was time for action.

"You seem to me a hale and hearty man, fully able to take care of yourself in a fair fight," he interjected from his post in the doorway. He and his mother had been listening to the protracted conversation from the next room, but he had moved into the entry a few minutes earlier to get a better view of the proceedings.

"Well, yes, of course, but . . ." Reynolds blustered, his face turning an even deeper shade of red than its apparently natural hue.

"Then all is arranged. Will you be so kind as to visit Miss Scott's aunts to explain the situation, and to have her servants pack suitable attire for her journey?" Spencer strolled into the room. "I shall have one of our footmen collect it in a plain black coach."

"How am I to know what is suitable? Will Elizabeth be staying in the country, or in the city? Will she be in the north, where the climate is so much harsher? I think I need to know that." Spencer detected a slight smile of victory playing about the other man's lips. He did not know why Reynolds was so determined to discover Miss Scott's destination, but that very determination warned Spencer not to give an inch.

"I think you should simply ask the servants to pack a wardrobe suitable to any situation. Surely that is not too much to ask."

Reynolds puffed out his breath. "Don't patronize me,

young man. Just because you're a fancy nob doesn't mean you can push me around."

"Please, Mr. Willoughby . . ." Miss Scott began.

Spencer cut her off, hating himself for his rudeness but determined to be rid of this pushy man of whom Miss Scott was so inexplicably fond. "I am not pushing you around," he told Reynolds, sensing that he had overplayed his hand slightly. "It is simply that Miss Scott has complete confidence in your ability to handle her affairs, and so do I."

The older man straightened up at this patent flattery. "Well, of course, I am well able to carry out any task she assigns me. And if she insists on this ridiculous course of hiding herself away, I shall do my best to keep the business prospering in her absence. But don't think I won't be keeping the Rivertons' man of business occupied with messages," he warned Miss Scott over Spencer's shoulder. "You are vital to the success of Roger Scott Importing, and I'll be demmed if I'll let this company fall into ruin simply because you've taken some foolish feminine notion into your head."

Inwardly, Spencer groaned. If anything could persuade Miss Scott to stay in London, it was the insinuation that her business would collapse without her. To his surprise, however, Miss Scott parried this latest thrust with ease.

"I know you value the business as much as I, Gerald. That is why I am comfortable leaving it in your capable hands." She moved across the room to give the older man a hug. "I would appreciate it if you could visit my aunts as quickly as possible. We must make an early start tomorrow, and it would set my mind at ease to have my trunks packed and ready. And thank you so much for all you have done." She flashed him a warm smile that twisted Spencer's gut with an uncustomary stab of envy. How he wished that smile were meant for him!

Any thoughts of smiles from Miss Scott were quickly

dispatched, however, after they had finally bid Reynolds good day.

"That was a most unpleasant interview," she remarked, returning to her seat by the fire. "I warned you that it would be difficult for me to pick up and leave my affairs."

Spencer felt a spark of irritation. He was grateful that he had convinced his mother to remain in the other room, so that he could have a somewhat private conversation with Miss Scott. "I am not disrupting your life merely for my own amusement. In case you have forgotten, I am trying to help you."

Miss Scott did not look at him, staring instead at the rosy coals in the grate. As he waited for her to respond, he looked about the room, trying to see it as she might see it.

It was not an interior designed to impress. While scrupulously neat—much more tidy than the rooms of many of his bachelor friends, he thought—it was somewhat austere. The threadbare rug before the fire was long past its fashionable days, and the burgundy leather of the twin wing chairs that flanked the hearth was cracked and worn. He had never given much thought to his furnishings. Now, for the first time he could recall, he wished he had paid more attention to them.

"I have not forgotten that you are helping me," Miss Scott finally replied. "Believe me, I am truly grateful for all that you and your family have done. I am simply not used to depending on anyone to this extent, especially strangers."

At her forlorn tone, Spencer chided himself for his abruptness. Seeking to lighten the atmosphere, he said, "Well, now is a very good time to start. We all have your best interests at heart—I, my family, and Mr. Reynolds."

"Yes, I know." Her voice was distant, as though she did not really believe what she was saying.

Whom does she doubt? Spencer wondered. *Me, or Reynolds?* Mentally, he added the avuncular Gerald Reynolds to his list of characters worthy of a bit of covert investigation.

Three

"As much as I adore London, it will be lovely to experience spring in the country for a change. Sometimes, I find the intensity of the Season a bit too much," Lady Riverton confessed.

"And although each of our estates is special, I must admit that I love Linden Park best." She turned away from the verdant fields outside the carriage window, and looked at Elizabeth. "We shall be there shortly, my dear. I hope the journey has not been too tiring?"

"Not at all. I have enjoyed our conversation so much that the time seems to have flown by," Elizabeth replied.

She truly had enjoyed chatting with Mr. Willoughby's mother, despite the older woman's astonishing ability to pepper her with endless questions. Elizabeth felt as though she had turned her entire life inside out for inspection. Well, perhaps not her entire life. She had regaled Lady Riverton with tales of her two rather eccentric aunts, talked about her interest in Herr von Beethoven's music, and even described her company's latest efforts to raise extra investment capital—a topic she guiltily suspected had bored her kind companion to distraction. Fortunately, however, she had managed to skirt most discussion of Victor and his unsettling hold over her.

Not willing to take a chance that Lady Riverton would

venture into this territory, Elizabeth renewed her efforts
to turn the conversation away from herself.

"Who will be at Linden Park when we arrive?" she
asked.

"I am not entirely certain," Lady Riverton confessed.
"Lord Riverton shall be there, of course; he rarely comes
to London. I could not even prevail upon him to attend
dear Matthew's wedding, as my husband is a country
man at heart.

"Our second eldest, Benjamin, takes after him, and
he has been working on several projects at Linden Park,
so I expect he will be in residence as well. We may not
see him right away, though." She laughed. "I am certain
he will be out in the fields or ensconced in the estate
office with his head buried in some agricultural text
when we arrive.

"His older brother, George, has been concerned about
some crops that were not doing well at Aldcross Hall,
our property in Buckinghamshire. So he will likely be
there, working with the tenants to uncover the problem."

"Your sons seem to take a very personal approach to
estate management," Elizabeth replied, failing to keep a
note of surprise out of her voice.

"They are both highly skilled at it. Our properties
have prospered well under their care. That is why Richard, our third son, felt confident in buying a commis-
sion—he knew all was well on the home front."

"And where is he now?"

"En route to a new posting in the Canadas. Someplace
with a peculiar name . . . Quebec, I believe. I was heartbroken to see him posted so far from home, but at least
the war there is over. I worried every night he was in
Spain."

"He came back unharmed?"

"Completely. He has always been a charmed young
man, thank heaven."

Elizabeth stretched her feet in front of her, flexing them to relieve some of the stiffness from the long journey. "And young Mr. Willoughby?" she asked. "Does he help your other two sons on the estates?"

Lady Riverton's forehead wrinkled as she considered the question. "Well, there isn't really much for him to do. Benjamin has Linden Park well in hand, while George handles all the important affairs at Aldcross Hall. Our other estates are very small."

"But surely your sons cannot run the properties alone?" Elizabeth asked, acutely aware of her ignorance of country estate management.

"No, of course not, my dear. But each property has an excellent manager, and there are many servants and tenants to keep them running smoothly. Spencer has no responsibilities in that regard."

Now it was Elizabeth's turn to be puzzled. "What are his interests, then?"

"Oh, Spencer is such a good boy. He is the life and soul of any party, and is always around to complete a table of whist."

Elizabeth's heart sank. She had so enjoyed Mr. Willoughby's company in London, and his genuine interest in helping her solve her problems. Was he nothing more than an indolent aristocrat, living off the hard work of his brothers and tenants?

"He does potter around a bit in the barn on some odd projects," Lady Riverton added. "Several times he has tried to explain them to me, but I am at a bit of a loss to understand them. He has always been this way, playing with bits of wood and pieces of twine. So unlike the other boys."

Lady Riverton's indulgent tone—almost the sort of voice one would use to talk about a sweet but deranged child—seemed completely unsuited to describing the dashing, intelligent man Elizabeth had encountered in

London. Uncertain how to proceed with the odd turn the conversation had taken, she asked the first question that popped into her head. "Did he consider following his brother into the army?"

"Oh my goodness, yes! When Richard joined up, Spencer was avid to do the same. But I just could not stomach the thought of two of my boys facing death overseas. My husband and I convinced him to put aside that foolish notion.

"Then he got it into his head that he should join the clergy," she continued. "Of all the preposterous ideas! Can you see Spencer as a country vicar?"

Elizabeth had to confess that she could not.

"With the help of our own vicar, we talked him out of that idea as well."

Perhaps he was somewhat weak-willed, but Elizabeth could not help but feel sorry for the gentleman whose family seemed determined to thwart his every ambition. "Poor Mr. Willoughby!" she cried before she had time to think how rude it would sound.

And, indeed, Lady Riverton blinked in confusion.

"What I mean is, he must be—must be—frustrated at not finding an occupation in life," Elizabeth stammered.

Lady Riverton drummed her fingers against the rich red velvet upholstery of her seat. "I have never really considered that before," she replied after a pause. "Spencer has always been simply Spencer. I have never really thought that he needed an occupation. We have an ample, if not huge, income, and Spencer's quarterly portion is sufficient to allow him to keep his rooms in St. James's. I do wonder whether we should look at raising his portion, however. He has always managed his funds well, but Benjamin seems to think he has been living rather close to his means lately. And his rooms do seem a trifle shabby."

Elizabeth's sympathy for the charming Mr. Wil-

loughby began to seep away. In her experience, there was
one primary reason why a previously prosperous man's
pockets were suddenly to let: gambling.

She sighed with disappointment. Fortunately, at that
moment the carriage rattled over a rough wooden bridge,
the noise making further comment impossible. When all
was quiet again, Elizabeth deftly turned the discussion
into less depressing channels.

Within the hour, they arrived at the massive stone
gates of Linden Park.

"My goodness, it is certainly impressive!" Elizabeth
exclaimed as the driver stopped the carriage to speak to
the gatekeeper.

"Oh, do not let the entrance intimidate you, my dear.
It is a relic from the days when the lord of Linden Park
owned many hundreds of acres in this part of Staffordshire. Most of that land was sold off long ago, and the
house that accompanied it burned to the ground when
my husband's father was a child. Our home is now a
more modest property than the gates would imply."

When the house in question hove into view at the end
of a sweeping drive lined with the property's namesake
linden trees, Elizabeth saw that Lady Riverton's definition of "modest" might differ from that of most people.
Linden Park, while not enormous, was nonetheless spacious and pleasingly proportioned. A domed circular portico with gleaming white columns stood out in an
otherwise ruthlessly symmetrical facade, whose two stories of mullioned windows twinkled in the sunlight. Two
wings swept back from the main section of the house,
and behind the nearest one Elizabeth glimpsed a terraced
garden. Altogether, it seemed a most pleasant place to
rusticate.

As the carriage pulled up to the portico, the front door
opened and two middle-aged men emerged. One, a small

gentleman wearing an impeccable dark coat, opened the carriage door and lowered the steps.

"Good afternoon, Lady Riverton," he said, holding out his hand to help that lady descend. "Welcome home."

"Thank you, Stevens," she replied as she dropped lightly to the ground. "Allow me to present Lady Mary Dixon, the daughter of my distant cousin Fanny."

"Welcome to Linden Park, Lady Mary," replied the butler. "Lady Riverton had sent word ahead that you would be staying with us. I hope you enjoy your time at Linden Park."

"I am sure I shall, thank you," said Elizabeth, unnerved by the butler's use of her fictitious title. She, Mr. Willoughby, and Lady Riverton had chosen her alias carefully. Mary had been Elizabeth's mother's name. Her absentminded father had addressed his daughter thus many times by mistake, so she was somewhat used to responding to it.

However, neither Lady Riverton nor Mr. Willoughby had informed her that she was to be a "lady" as well. She did not like it, but it was too late to go back.

She descended from the carriage steps to observe Lady Riverton emerging from a warm embrace with a tall, slim gentleman whose hair might once have been blond but had now faded to a pale, shimmering gray.

"Lady Mary, please allow me to introduce you to my husband, Lord Riverton," her companion said, drawing that gentleman forward.

"I'm afraid Benjamin is out in the fields," Lord Riverton apologized with a rueful grin that reminded Elizabeth strongly of Spencer Willoughby's. "He shall join us for dinner, however."

The party moved up the wide stone stairs and entered the house. The foyer, like the home's exterior, was both elegant and understated, with a floor of black-and-white tiles and walls of a deep golden hue. An enormous portrait of a young blond woman wearing a lace-festooned gown dominated the entryway.

"My husband's mother," Lady Riverton said, following Elizabeth's gaze. "The portrait was one of the few items saved from the fire."

"She is lovely," Elizabeth said, reflecting as she spoke that when the picture was painted, two generations ago, her own forebears were still running motley market stalls in Covent Garden and had little money to spare for portraits.

"I'm sure you would like some time to recover from the journey, Lady Mary." Lady Riverton interrupted her self-deprecating thoughts. "Nellie will show you to your room."

As a quiet young housemaid led her up the Persian-carpeted staircase, Elizabeth thought that she would need quite a bit of time to recover from a journey that had changed her in less than two days from Miss Elizabeth Scott, importer and fugitive, to Lady Mary Dixon, woman of leisure.

Spencer strolled through the arcaded courtyard of the Royal Exchange, trading greetings with several acquaintances. Although he was much more familiar with the hurly-burly of the newer Stock Exchange in Throgmorton Street, the stockbrokers who raised capital over there often had occasion to approach the wealthy merchants and traders here in order to assess their interest in investing a few pounds in a new venture. And the Royal, of course, would be the place where both Victor Newfield and Gerald Reynolds would do business.

"Hallo, Spence!" A smiling man in his early thirties, whose flaming red hair and freckles made him look scarcely older than a schoolboy, hurried over to shake Spencer's hand.

"Patrick, good to see you. How is business?"

"Same as ever, same as ever," the Irishman replied. "Too many cautious people afraid to look boldly into the future. But a few brave souls believe, and that's all I need. What are ye doin' over here, man? There's naught here to invest in but a few rugs and bolts of cloth."

"I could ask the same of you." Spencer laughed.

"Ah, I'm here looking for some wealthy ones eager to put their funds into the latest steam technology. There's a bright young man up north working on a machine that could change the whole industry of mining. If he's right, there may soon be no need to send the wee lads down into the tunnels. It could all be done by machine!"

"That is something I would be most interested in discussing further. It is a complete disgrace that so many children are ruining their health before they have even had a chance to grow," said Spencer. "But, sadly, my pockets are a bit to let at the minute."

"Aye, I know how it is." The red-haired man nodded. "Are ye still seeking investors for those picture experiments?"

Spencer gave a resigned sigh. It seemed he was always looking for funds for his work. "Yes, but that is not why I am here. I am looking for a bit of information today—strictly confidential, you understand?"

Patrick nodded again. "No sense letting everyone know your business, I always say."

"Exactly. I was wondering whether you might know something about one of the merchants here—a man named Victor Newfield. He owns a large drapery in the Strand."

"Ah, that one." Patrick frowned. "I tried to interest him in that steam-engine mining proposal a few months back. I had thought he would be a fine choice, owning such a prosperous-looking firm and all. But he told me he had no ready blunt at all, not a pound. I imagined he was just trying to get rid of me, but when I asked around, I heard the gossip: he's in debt for something like ten thousand pounds. Can't keep away from the gaming tables."

This information confirmed what Elizabeth had said.

"One of his largest creditors is a mill owner named Henry Cox, who has a small office in Cannon Street. He could tell you much more about Newfield than I could, but I believe I heard that he is away in Manchester for a few days, visiting his factory there."

"Thank you for the information." Spencer made a mental note to call upon Mr. Cox's offices later in the week.

"Rather than investing, Newfield asked me to help him raise some money, but I wouldn't go near him," the Irishman continued. "Nor would most of the other brokers. No one wants to put their clients' funds into a gambler's hands. You might as well throw it right in the Thames."

True enough, Spencer thought. "Did he seem desperate?"

"Aye. He had that look in his eyes of a man about to go before the firing squad. Panicked." Patrick gave a humorless chuckle. "And well he might be, unlucky man. If he doesn't get himself out of debt soon, he's likely off to Fleet Prison."

"Can you tell me what he looks like?"

"Sure, you can't miss him. Tall lad, must be over six feet. Dark hair, rather unkempt. Bit sallow-looking." Patrick swept his eyes around the sunny courtyard. "Haven't seen him here today, though. You'll probably stand a better chance of finding him in his offices."

"I may just do that," Spencer replied with studied carelessness. "What about a man named Gerald

Reynolds? Do you know anything of him? He is a manager with Roger Scott Importing."

Patrick paused, scratching his head. "Not much. I don't know him, myself. Bit of a temper on him, from what I've heard. Seems he was furious that Scott didn't make him a partner in the firm. The old man died a few months back, and the daughter inherited the lot. Can you imagine! The business, the ships, the house, everything—gone to a young lass. They say she's quite the pretty one," he mused.

"So I've heard," murmured Spencer, a sudden vision of Elizabeth's soft, shiny curls popping into his brain.

They exchanged a few more pleasantries, then Patrick hurried off to meet with a coal exporter who might be interested in his steam-engine scheme.

Spencer, curious to discover more about the penniless Victor, collected his horse and headed west toward Newfield's shop in the Strand. With luck, he would be able to spot Elizabeth's tormentor leaving his premises on his way to somewhere interesting.

As Spencer arrived in the Strand, he saw that Patrick was right; Newfield and Son certainly looked prosperous. Two bow windows filled with rich-looking fabrics framed a large oak door. A group of older women, deep in a conversation punctuated by raucous laughter, entered the shop. This gave him a glimpse of the spacious interior, its walls lined with bolts of cloth.

Not wanting to be seen too close to Newfield's premises, Spencer settled into a small coffeehouse across the street. He had just had time to drink half of a small cup of coffee when he saw two men emerging from a door that apparently led to the offices above the shop. The tall, gangly one had a mop of shaggy black hair.

Aha, there you are, Spencer thought, draining his cup and placing it back on its chipped china saucer. But when he recognized the second gentleman, he almost choked.

The portly figure waving his arms at Newfield in a most agitated manner was Gerald Reynolds.

Spencer shot to his feet in a spurt of anger at the sight of Miss Scott's manager. Hurrying out of the coffeeshop, he concealed himself in a doorway to watch the rest of the exchange. Given the noise of passing carriages, he could not hear a word of their conversation, but Newfield's scowl made it plain that it was not a pleasant one. After a few more angry comments, Reynolds turned his back on the younger man and strode down the street.

Spencer consciously tamped down his fury and debated his next move. He had several options.

It appeared that Reynolds was acting as Newfield's spy. One possible course of action open to Spencer would involve confronting Newfield in his office and dissuading him—somehow—from following Miss Scott to Linden Park.

Spencer dismissed that idea on two counts. First, if Reynolds was simply discussing some business matter with Newfield, and had not revealed Miss Scott's connection to the Rivertons, Spencer's sudden appearance at Newfield's office might give the game away. Second, Spencer realized with a familiar sense of defeat, Newfield had a good six inches and three stone on him. In any kind of physical confrontation, Spencer was certain to lose—just as surely as he had always lost any sort of fight against his older brothers when he was a child, and just as he had been the easy target of every bully at Harrow. It was no wonder that his brother Richard had laughed at his notion of joining the army, Spencer thought for the millionth time.

No, as usual, he would have to rely on outsmarting his opponent rather than overpowering him. And to do that, he had to find out exactly what Newfield knew.

He turned back to the coffeehouse and settled down

for another cup. He wanted to give Reynolds plenty of time to get back to his office.

"May I speak with Mr. Reynolds, sir?" Spencer asked the harried young clerk sitting at a desk near the office's main door. The large room—sunny near the windows, somewhat dim in the center—was filled with similar clerks sitting at similar desks. Some were checking enormous ledgers, adding up sums on sheets of foolscap. Others were engaged in conversation with visitors. A heady aroma of coffee and cinnamon, possibly emanating from a stack of wooden crates in one corner of the otherwise neat office, permeated the establishment.

"May I tell him who is calling, sir?" The man looked hesitant.

"My name is Spencer Willoughby. I have a message from Miss Scott."

"Oh, Miss Scott! Well, that's all right then." The clerk sprang up to find the manager, who immediately appeared from an enclosed office at the back of the room.

"Ah, Mr. Willoughby! I did not expect to see you so soon! What brings you to our premises?" The florid man extended his hand in welcome, but Spencer noticed that his smile did not quite reach his eyes. Not surprising, given how rancorously they had parted last. Or could it be that he had something to hide?

"Nothing of great import, I must admit," he replied as they walked into Reynolds's office and closed the door behind them. "I was in the neighborhood, and I thought I would take the opportunity to pass along Miss Scott's gratitude for your work in handling her affairs. She was most pleased with the trunks her maids packed for her journey. She assured me that she had the utmost trust in you, and I see that it was not misplaced."

"Well, yes, thank you." The older man beamed,
pleased with the compliment.

"I also wanted to discuss a plan with you. I would
like a friend of mine to meet with Mr. Newfield. It
doesn't make sense for me to do it myself, of course—
that would make it possible for him to link me with Miss
Scott, and perhaps discover her location." Spencer noted
with grim satisfaction that a slow red flush began to
creep beneath Reynolds's white but inexpertly tied neckcloth.

"Perhaps my friend can get to the root of Newfield's
ridiculous actions and make him see reason," he continued. "Then Miss Scott could return to London quite
quickly."

Gerald Reynolds made no comment. Instead, he
moved idly about the room. He picked up an ivory-handled letter opener, looked at it as though he had never
seen it before, and put it down absently on a corner of
his desk.

"You wouldn't happen to know where I could find
Newfield's office, would you?" Spencer asked.

At the direct, innocuous question, Reynolds looked up.
"Well, yes, I believe his offices are above his shop in
the Strand."

"And would you know whether he is there today?"

The flush crept higher. "I am sure I would not, Mr.
Willoughby. I have not seen Mr. Newfield in several
weeks."

"Well, I suppose my friend will have to take his
chances, then," Spencer replied with false lightness. With
his lie, Reynolds proved that he was hiding his dealings
with Newfield. That meant he had told Newfield of
Elizabeth's flight, and of her connection to the Rivertons.

As he left the offices of Roger Scott Importing,
Spencer had to will himself not to run through the ani-
mated groups of traders thronging the street outside.

He had to get to Linden Park with all due haste. Reynolds might not have been able to tell Newfield exactly where Miss Scott had gone, but he had probably suggested that Victor visit one of the Rivertons' country estates.

Spencer devoutly hoped that Newfield decided to go to Aldcross Hall first.

Four

Elizabeth helped herself to some eggs from the sideboard and settled alone at the table in the breakfast room of Linden Park. It was after ten in the morning, but there was no sign of anyone on the ground floor of the house, save the footman who had brought her a cup of chocolate.

What a life it must be, Elizabeth thought as she reached for a muffin from a basket on the table. *One could sleep until noon without a care in the world.*

"Good morning, Lady Mary." The quiet voice of Mr. Willoughby's older brother interrupted her musings.

"Good morning," Elizabeth said with guilty surprise, as Benjamin Willoughby seated himself at the table. "You are up and about early this morning."

Benjamin, five years older than his brother Spencer, was a tall, rangy man with callused hands and a cautious smile. When she had been introduced to him the previous evening, Elizabeth had had trouble believing he was even related to the younger Mr. Willoughby. But Benjamin had a sweet, muted version of Spencer's ebullient charm, and she had warmed to him immediately.

"Early!" He laughed as he drew the basket of muffins toward him and extracted three. "I have been up since six. There is a fence in the east field that needed mending." For the first time, she noticed the bits of mud smearing his cuffs, which peeked out from the sleeve of the clean jacket he had obviously just donned, and detected a faint whiff of the barn.

"I thought you might be awake, and I decided to take a break to keep you company," he continued, dusting the first muffin with sugar from a muffineer. "Father is in the village meeting with the vicar about repairs to the church roof, and I knew Mother would not be stirring for hours."

"Ah, you underestimate me, Benjamin." Lady Riverton swept into the room.

"Good morning, Mother." Benjamin rose and kissed his mother on the cheek. "To what do we owe your early appearance?"

"You are not the only one with manners, you impudent pup," Lady Riverton said, moving to the sideboard. "I thought Miss . . . er . . . Lady Mary might enjoy a little conversation with her breakfast." She settled at the table with her plate. "Did you sleep well, Lady Mary?"

Elizabeth was slowly becoming used to her new form of address, although the thought of posing as a member of the nobility continued to disturb her. "Very well, thank you. But I am sorry you have risen early on my behalf."

"Nonsense, my dear," replied Lady Riverton. "It is time I started keeping proper country hours. And I am glad for the company. Benjamin does not usually see fit to bless the house with his presence until dinner."

"Some of us must earn our keep, Mother." Benjamin smiled, then bit hungrily into his muffin.

"And you do so, marvelously," Lady Riverton said. "And, now that you are here, perhaps you have some ideas about how we could help Lady Mary resolve her dilemma?"

Last evening, to Elizabeth's discomfort, the family had discussed her dilemma in great detail. Lord Riverton and Benjamin had been told her real name, but they had all agreed to use her assumed name so that she could get used to it. After all, it could be weeks before she could return home, so she had to adjust to her secret identity. It seemed silly, so far from London, but Elizabeth supposed the Rivertons were right. It did no harm to be cautious. If she had to answer to a ridiculous aristocratic title for a few days to stay safe from Victor, she would do so. It was a small price to pay.

"Well, one thing did occur to me while I was looking through the tack in the stables this morning," Benjamin ventured, as he rose to get another helping of eggs from the sideboard. "I know this sounds impertinent, Lady Mary, but could you possibly escape your situation by simply marrying someone else?"

At this suggestion, Elizabeth let out the first genuine laugh she had enjoyed in weeks. Benjamin looked chagrined.

"It is not impertinent at all, Mr. Willoughby!" she hastened to reassure him. "I laughed only because it is so unlikely. You see, I have never had much time to socialize, so the eligible men I meet are few. And, to be honest, no one except my revolting cousin—and fortune hunters like him—seems the least interested in winning the hand of a lady of business. Once gentlemen hear me discussing import taxes and market fluctuations, their slight interest in my feminine charms completely evaporates!"

Elizabeth stopped when she noticed the dismay on Lady Riverton's kind face. "Truly, Lady Riverton, I do not mind. I very much enjoy my work, and I have no desire to marry anyone who would make me give it up. And I am afraid just about every man in England would fall into that category." She sighed.

"But are you not lonely, my dear?" her hostess persisted. "With no immediate family, it must be a very quiet life."

Elizabeth pondered this as she sipped her chocolate. "I suppose it is. I have never given it much thought. But

I have my aunts for company, and my business to keep me busy. I have never been unhappy." A quick, vivid image of Spencer popped into her mind. Life would certainly not be dull with such a man around.

She quenched that thought. He was very charming, true, but he doubtless would have no interest in a mere cit—particularly if he knew the whole truth of her heritage. All in all, not a man for her.

"Lady Mary?" Benjamin was looking at her, his eyebrows raised, and she gave a small, guilty start.

"You must forgive me, Mr. Willoughby. I'm afraid I was woolgathering."

He gave her a gentle smile. "I am not at all surprised. You have a lot to think about at the minute. I was just bidding you good morning." He rose from the table and strode to the door. "I have much I need to accomplish by midday, as I must meet with the estate manager this afternoon. Enjoy the rest of your morning, Lady Mary. And good day, Mother."

Lady Riverton watched him go, then poured herself another cup of tea. "He does enjoy life in the country so," she remarked. "He is very much his father's son in that way."

"And his brother, the younger Mr. Willoughby? Is he a country man at heart too?" Elizabeth asked, then chided herself. Really, it was most unseemly, this interest she was showing in Spencer Willoughby.

If Lady Riverton found it untoward, however, she gave no sign. "Spencer enjoys the country, to be certain, although he is much more fond of city life than any of our other sons. He is mad for the theater, and he also enjoys the odd game of chance, I know."

Elizabeth gave a tiny sigh. In her experience, young men did not enjoy "the odd game" when it came to gambling. One game quickly became several, and several quickly became a three-day disaster.

And yet, Elizabeth couldn't seem to keep the questions from coming. "And when he is here, does he assist Benjamin with the work around the estate?"

"Oh yes, he enjoys working outdoors when he has the opportunity. And, of course, he works in the barn." Lady Riverton nibbled at her toast, but did not elaborate.

"In the barn?" Elizabeth was acutely aware of her ignorance of country life. What on earth was he doing in the barn—repairing tack, perhaps?

"Oh, tinkering with some outlandish thing or another," Lady Riverton replied. "He has a corner where he keeps his bits of tin and sacks of powders. I used to be terrified he would ignite the whole barn, but he assures me that it is all perfectly safe, so I try not to bother him about it. Truth to tell, I am not at all certain what he is doing."

Elizabeth was intrigued. Whatever could Mr. Willoughby be engaged in? She found Lady Riverton's vagueness somewhat irritating, and resolved to ask Spencer about his activities when next they met.

She found herself hoping she would have the opportunity to see him again soon.

Agitated after sitting indoors all morning with nothing to occupy her mind, Elizabeth set off after nuncheon for a long walk about the property. Linden Park was set in a small, lovely valley, and its green fields stretched away in all directions. In the distance, the spire of the village church poked up through a stand of trees. Following a path along the river, she soon reached the tiny village, which consisted of several rows of prosperous-looking cottages, a squat stone mill, two shops, and the church.

As she passed one of the shops, she noticed a small child tugging on his mother's skirt.

"Mum, look, look at the lady! I don't know that lady!" he cried.

The young mother hurriedly shushed the little boy. "Pardon me, miss, he's just young and his manners aren't quite the best yet." She gave Elizabeth an embarrassed smile.

"Oh, I think his manners are just fine." She knelt down until she was at the toddler's eye level. "I'm sorry, I should have introduced myself," she said gravely. "I'm Miss . . . Lady Mary Dixon. And may I have the pleasure of knowing your name?"

The towheaded child twisted back and forth, then hid his head in his mother's skirts with a giggle.

"Now, young Tom, don't be rude." Tom's mother gave his hand a gentle shake. "Say hello."

Shyly, the lad turned to face her. "Hello. I'm Thomas Simpson."

"Well, hello, Master Simpson. And, Mrs. Simpson." She nodded at the young woman. "I am pleased to make your acquaintance."

"Likewise, m'lady." Mrs. Simpson bobbed a brief curtsy, an action that rather startled Elizabeth. "But we must not take up more of your time. Come along, Tom."

"G'day, miss," Tom piped up as they took their leave.

Miss. Elizabeth smiled as she walked in the other direction. The young lad had the right of it. She felt much more comfortable as a Miss than as grand Lady Mary.

She continued to think about the encounter as she made her way back to Linden Park along a quiet road. Young children never begged an introduction in London. But here, she realized, she was something of a curiosity. In a small country village, new faces would be cause for excitement. In London, unfamiliar faces were often all one saw in the course of a day walking about the city.

She inhaled deeply. Even the air was different here, scented as it was with the aromas of wildflowers and new grass. Living in London for so long, she had become used to the dank, close atmosphere in the city, redolent with the smells of too many people living too close together. The fresh, country air was invigorating, and she picked up her pace as she approached the house.

It was such a treat to wander about unchaperoned, she thought as she strolled up the lane. It was wise, she knew, not to travel London's streets alone, but she irrationally loathed society's requirement that she be watched like a wayward child wherever she went. And while she liked Jenny very much, her maid's endless stream of chatter could be enervating. The silence of a country walk was just what Elizabeth had needed to clear her cluttered mind.

Just before she reached the manicured park, she heard the beat of hooves behind her—the sound of a mounted rider approaching at a swift pace. A needle of fear pierced her. Surely Victor could not have found her so quickly?

She chided herself for her folly. Of course her cousin could not have located her. She had done everything possible to hide her whereabouts. Panicking at every small sound was pointless. Forcing herself to be calm, she turned to look at the approaching rider—and immediately smiled.

Even at a distance, his shock of fair hair gave Spencer Willoughby away. The wave of excitement that washed over Elizabeth as she recognized him caught her by surprise. Goodness, she was glad to see him. But what had brought him back from London so soon?

She stopped by the side of the lane and watched him approach. He cut a very fine figure in the saddle, she had to admit, with his royal blue riding habit and tall beaver hat. Horse and rider seemed to move with one fluid motion as they cantered up the lane. She could not take her eyes from the graceful pair—indeed, she was mortified to find herself staring as Mr. Willoughby drew up beside her and brought his mount to a halt.

"Good work, Star," he murmured to the horse as he dropped lightly to the ground. "And good day, Miss Scott. Oh, my apologies. I mean, Lady Mary."

"Good day, Mr. Willoughby. What a pleasure to see you." She could feel a faint flush rising to her cheeks. How embarrassing, to be blushing like a schoolgirl!

"What brings you home so soon from London?" she continued doggedly, hoping he would attribute her pink cheeks to the exertion of her walk.

He took the horse's bridle in his hand and began to walk at an easy pace. She fell into step behind him.

"I wish my errand were a happier one, but I am afraid I have some disturbing news to share." She glanced at his handsome profile and for the first time noticed the furrow of worry between his brows.

"There is no pleasant way to tell you this, so I shall be blunt. Your manager, Mr. Reynolds, appears to be in the employ of Victor Newfield." He stopped to look at her, his gaze appearing to assess her reaction.

She struggled to keep the panic she felt from showing on her face. "Whatever do you mean? Gerald has always been most loyal to my family."

"Sadly, I am afraid that his loyalty now belongs to your cousin. I saw him deep in conversation with Mr. Newfield in the Strand. Yet when I approached him later that day, he denied any contact with Victor."

"Gerald, betray me? I cannot fathom it." Elizabeth shook her head, the pleasure of her country walk evaporating in an instant. Suddenly, London and its attendant worries seemed all too close. "Well, that settles it. I must return to London at once."

"Return to London? But you will not be safe there!"

"It appears I am not safe here, either. Blast bloody Victor!" she cried, then blushed again, this time with chagrin. "My apologies, Mr. Willoughby. Having spent too much time around the docks, I am afraid my vocabulary is sometimes most unsuitable for a lady."

To her amazement, he chuckled. "Your language is entirely appropriate to the situation. I should like to blast bloody Victor myself."

She laughed, too, but her amusement soon faded. "In all seriousness, though, I should return to London. If Victor has been able to hoodwink even Gerald, he may well have contacts in my household too. I am deeply afraid for my aunts' welfare—I must return to them at once."

Spencer smiled, and she marveled at the way that expression lit up his whole face. "On that score, my lady, I have already beaten you to the punch."

"Beaten me to the punch?"

"A boxing expression. Forgive me. What I meant to say was that I have already thought ahead and have taken measures to bring your aunts here to Linden Park. They should arrive by tomorrow at the latest, in the company of two of our most dire-looking footmen. I would have accompanied them myself, but I wanted to ride ahead to ensure that you were safe. And, I am glad to see, you are." His gentle tone warmed Elizabeth right down to her toes, as did his concern for her welfare. But his next words dispersed that glow.

"I am afraid, however, that I must caution you against taking any more unaccompanied walks around the property in the future. We cannot know what Mr. Reynolds has told your cousin, and I cannot risk having him scoop you up from some isolated country lane."

Elizabeth stifled the urge to bridle at his peremptory order. After all, his reasoning was absolutely sound. Had she not been worried about just such a disaster only five minutes before? And now, the possibility was much more real.

"You are right, of course," she said. "And thank you

most kindly for arranging for my aunts to come to Linden Park. I do so loathe being an imposition." Much as she liked the Rivertons, and Spencer particularly, Elizabeth admitted that it galled her on a fundamental level to find herself beholden to an aristocratic family. Cits and nobles simply were not meant to mix.

But Spencer was waving away her concern. "It is no imposition whatsoever, I can assure you. As you can see, Linden Park is a great rambling heap of a place. There are probably guest rooms tucked away in wings I've no idea even exist. And my mother will be over the moon to have more guests to indulge—particularly two ladies close to her own age."

"I must thank you, Mr. Willoughby. Even with the house heavily guarded, I was most worried about my aunts in London. It will be a relief to have them here. But if Victor appears . . ."

"Do not worry about that just yet," Mr. Willoughby cut in. He slowed his pace as they approached the barn, and a young groom bounded toward them. Her companion passed Star's bridle to the lad and thanked him, then turned toward the house.

"We have a number of properties, and this one is one of the more distant ones from London," Spencer reassured her. "Mr. Reynolds had no way of knowing where exactly we were going. It will likely be days before Victor ascertains your whereabouts. And by that time, if we are fortunate, your legal affairs will be in order and you will be safe from your cousin's demands."

He paused, then continued. "If I may broach one more idea, Lady Mary, I would like to suggest that your lawyer turn over your papers to our man of business. He can bring them to our solicitor, who can come here to work out the fine details with you."

"But why should that be necessary?" Elizabeth asked. "My solicitor has worked with my family for many years and is intimately familiar with our affairs. A stranger will not have that advantage."

Spencer hesitated again. "I dislike being so cautious, but I am concerned that Victor may have some sort of link to your solicitor as well."

"Of course." Silently, Elizabeth berated herself for her shortsightedness. If Victor could turn Gerald Reynolds against her, there was no telling who else had fallen prey to his scheme. Was no one safe? Was there no one she could trust?

At the minute, it appeared she had no one but Spencer and his family, she reflected as they walked under the portico. And why she trusted him, she could not say. Perhaps it was feminine folly.

She nibbled on her lower lip as she thought through the problem. Then, catching a glimpse of Mr. Willoughby's kind, worried face, she pasted what she hoped was a sunny smile on her own visage and followed him into the cool, elegant foyer of Linden Park.

Five

Spencer pried open the lid of a tin of muriatic acid, wincing as an acrid smell assaulted his nostrils. He tipped a small portion of the liquid into a small vial. After noting the quantity in a spattered notebook, he added the liquid to a large beaker of water.

He poured the resulting solution into a flat metal pan, taking care not to splash any onto his hands. Even though he wore thick work gloves, he knew from experience that the fabric would not completely protect his skin from the corrosive acid.

After rocking the pan back and forth carefully to ensure that the liquid was evenly distributed, he opened a lead-lined box beneath his worktable and extracted a small, flat piece of leather. Most of the leather, originally white, was now black. But in the center of the piece was the pale outline of a leaf, several of its ribs visible. It had taken him days to get such a clear image.

With a smooth, swift movement, he thrust the image into the pan of fixative. It was crucial to submerge the image quickly, before the light from the large window above his head could affect it.

He held his breath. This solution of muriatic acid would work, he was certain of it. It had to work soon. His funds were almost gone, and without the prospect of imminent success, it would be demmed hard to solicit more. His last investor had left in disgust at the lack of progress. If only nitrate of silver weren't so dear.

He continued to rock the pan gently, willing the submerged image to remain clear. Humphrey Davy and others had been experimenting with various chemicals in an attempt to keep sun-exposed images from fading, and Spencer was convinced that his own approach stood a good chance at success. It had to work.

But after a few minutes, the image had begun to turn gray. Within a quarter of an hour, only a faint brown vestige of the leaf's outline remained on the leather, which had turned almost completely black.

Spencer groaned with frustration and leaned his head against the small shelf he had built over his worktable. Why? What had gone wrong this time? Why couldn't he find the answer, after all these months?

Willing the unproductive thoughts away, he pushed himself away from the shelf and reached for his notebook again. "May 12, 1818: No success. Suspect that a stronger concentration of acid will improve results," he wrote.

So absorbed was he in his notes that he did not hear Benjamin approaching. "How is your work coming?" his brother asked as he entered the tiny workroom.

"A few steps forward, a few steps back," Spencer replied, reluctant to admit his lack of progress even to Ben. Especially to Ben.

"It certainly smells portentous," Benjamin added, folding his long legs beneath him as he settled onto the room's only seating, a battered old milking stool. "If the picture making doesn't succeed, perhaps you could set up a profitable still."

"These solutions are rather more lethal than even old Carson's moonshine," he replied, remembering the illegal potions brewed by an elderly tenant with which he and his brothers had experimented in their foolish youth.

"True. But perhaps there is some other use to which you could put them."

Spencer gritted his teeth. He was interested in only one use for these materials. And it would work. Eventually.

"Perhaps," he replied in a neutral voice.

"I must confess, the intent of this work still eludes me," Benjamin said, stripping off his heavy work gloves and flicking them against his knee to shake off the dust. "What, exactly, are you working on today?"

"I am trying to come up with the right proportions of the correct chemicals to concoct a workable fixative."

"But that is what I do not understand. How does liquid affect the image?"

Spencer grinned, warming to his subject. "Remember when I explained that I treat the pieces of leather with a substance called nitrate of silver?"

Benjamin nodded.

"The silver nitrate becomes black when exposed to sunlight," Spencer explained. "However, if I place something on top of the treated leather—such as a leaf, or a scrap of lace—that object blocks the light, to some extent."

"You have explained this to me before. That is how you obtain the white images on the leather, is it not?"

"Yes."

"But the problem is that, once you remove the object, you cannot stop the silver from reacting to light?"

Spencer nodded. "What I am attempting to do is to find a chemical that will react with the nitrate of silver and cause it to lose its sensitivity to light. If that can be done, the image could be preserved indefinitely."

"I think I see." Benjamin paused, his forehead furrowed. "But how can you know which chemicals will work? Are there not hundreds of compounds?"

"Thousands," Spencer agreed. "But many have known

properties, and scientists are discovering more about them every day. The range of elements and compounds most likely to fix the image is actually quite limited. I am focusing on one—muriatic acid—that I am convinced will work, if I can find the correct concentration."

"But then what?" Ben asked.

"What do you mean?"

"What will be the use of the process when you are done?"

Spencer suppressed a sigh of frustration. He was very fond of his brother, but Ben had no use for any technology that did not relate to plows or horses.

"If it works—when it works—we will be able to reproduce completely accurate images of anything we choose."

"But are not painters able to do that already?" Ben picked up a small measuring spoon, turning it over in his hand curiously.

"They can make images, certainly, but they can never completely capture a real object in all its infinite detail," Spencer replied. "My experiments are crude, I am the first to admit. But there are some scientists who believe that photographic techniques could one day be used with a camera obscura to reproduce images of much larger things."

He leaned back against his worktable, his earlier frustration with his experiments forgotten as he tried to communicate his enthusiasm for optics to his brother.

"We might be able to make pictures of animals in far-off places, for instance, allowing scientists here to study their features without risking the animals' lives to bring them to England. We could distribute exact likenesses of missing people throughout the country, helping others locate them." Thinking briefly of Elizabeth, he conceded that this might not always be an advantage.

"But of what use is it to you personally?" Ben persisted. "You are not a tradesman. You do not wish to sell such equipment, do you?"

"Eventually, yes." Spencer smothered another sigh. This was an old argument between him and his sibling.

"But such endeavors are fleeting. They are not a wise basis for future prosperity. Not for a lifetime, or for one's descendants."

"Seeing as I have no descendants, that is hardly an issue." Spencer turned away and glanced into his tray, on the chance that even a faint trace of the image remained on the leather. There was nothing left.

"But that may not always be the case. Spence, the only true source of wealth is land. You would be wise to start saving your funds to invest in an estate of your own."

"Ben, I could put aside my allowance for twenty years, and I would be unlikely to be able to afford a property of any scale. And, truly, I have no interest in such a plan. Land has been the source of wealth in England for many generations," he admitted. "But the world is changing, Ben. Investigations such as mine are going to alter our lives completely. Already, steam engines are doing the work of twenty men in the mines, and mechanical looms are producing more cloth in a day than a team of skilled weavers was once able to produce in a month. What will happen when devices such as these begin to take over the work of reapers and plows?"

"It will not happen," Ben said with conviction. "Those things happen in cities, not here."

"They will happen here," Spencer cried in frustration. "They are already happening here. And the city has already begun to touch the country. Did you not say that Will Kerr's two sons have gone to Manchester, to work in the mills?"

"Well, yes, but they are just two feckless young lads. Always were."

"No, they are going where they are needed, and where they can earn enough money to support a family. There will be more like them—next week, next month, next year. Machines are the future, Ben. And I want to be a part of the future." He sighed. "There is no place for me in the past."

"I know I shall not change your mind on this issue, so I shall not try," Ben replied. "Instead, let me turn the topic to more congenial matters. I am greatly enjoying the company of Miss Scott—or Lady Mary, or whatever we are to call her. She is a most congenial houseguest."

Spencer smiled. "I did not know that you had even noticed her. Usually you remark only on horses, seeds, and the latest additions to Cook's repertoire."

His brother grinned back. "Too true, sadly. But even I would have to be blind not to notice Miss Scott. She is a very attractive young woman."

Spencer felt a prickle of irritation. "She is staying with us out of necessity, Ben. If you think she has any interest in meeting eligible gentleman farmers, you are sorely mistaken."

Ben gave his brother a shrewd look, his eyes narrowed. "What brought on this outburst, little brother? I simply noted that Miss Scott was lovely. I am not about to corner her in the conservatory and press my attentions on her."

Spencer said nothing for a moment. Why had he reacted so strongly? Ben's comment had been harmless, and a natural one in the circumstances.

He was attracted to Miss Scott himself, of course, but it was just a passing fancy. Like Ben, he had no desire or intention to court the young woman. He was in no position to court anyone, and if he were, he doubted that a rich, self-assured female such as Miss Scott would be his first choice.

"I do not know why I reacted so to your observation," he finally answered his brother. "I think my frustration with my afternoon's work has put me out of sorts. My apologies for venting my anger on you."

"Do not worry, Spence," Ben said, rising from his stool and gathering up his discarded gloves. "But if the optics work is not satisfying, why not stop? It pains me to see you wasting your energy and your intelligence in such pursuits."

And my inheritance, Spencer added silently, too proud to admit to his brother that his pockets were to let again. "I thank you for your concern, but truly, there is no need. When I succeed, you shall all be coming to me for your allowance!" he said, with forced lightness.

I will succeed, he thought as Ben left him alone with his blackened leather and almost-empty tins of chemicals. *When I do, I shall finally be able to hold up my head in this family.*

And, perhaps, think about a different sort of future for myself, as well.

With new resolve, he pulled his notebook toward himself and finished recording his observations of the day's experiment.

Six

Elizabeth scanned her closely written letter. The missive, to her friend Cassandra Baker and Cassandra's new husband, David, would likely come as something of a surprise to them both, as she was asking whether David Baker would agree to serving as the trustee for her estate.

She had met Mr. Baker several times and sensed he was an upstanding and honorable man, but they were not acquaintances of long standing. Her request would be unexpected, to say the least. However, she needed to find a trustee quickly, and any of her associates in London might have fallen under Victor's influence. She doubted, however, that Victor even knew of the Bakers, whose quiet estate in Yorkshire was far removed from the doings of the City. They rarely ventured to Town.

Satisfied that the letter outlined as much of her current situation as was necessary without giving any hint of her emotional distress, Elizabeth picked up a small container of fine sand and shook it over the drying ink.

It had been difficult to refrain from telling her friends the entire sorry tale. In particular, Elizabeth longed to share her worries about Aunt Louisa and Aunt Harriet. She knew it would take several days to convey the elderly ladies to Linden Park, but she would not rest easily until they had joined her again.

She was loath to voice her fears to the Rivertons, however, at the risk of appearing ungrateful for their assistance. She would simply have to be patient.

She cast a glance about the room. All the occupants appeared engrossed in their chosen activities. Lord Riverton was chortling over something he had read in the week-old London newspaper splayed on his lap. His wife was intent on a game of whist she was playing with Benjamin, a middle-aged neighbor named Mrs. Morrison, and Mrs. Morrison's rather skittish daughter, Annabel.

To her surprise, Spencer had not joined the boisterous card game. Instead, he was secluded in a corner by the fireplace, reading a worn leather-bound book. The lamplight glinted off his hair, giving him an almost angelic appearance. Elizabeth smiled at the thought. She suspected that Mr. Willoughby—with his fondness for the theater and his empty pockets—was far from an angel.

"You appear to have finished your correspondence," Lady Riverton remarked, looking up from her cards. "Are you certain you would not like to join us for a round of whist? Or perhaps piquet?"

"Quite certain," Elizabeth replied, folding her letter and applying a dab of sealing wax. "I am no hand at cards."

"We would be pleased to teach you," piped up Mrs. Morrison. "Truly, it does pass the time. And we play only for pennies. You needn't fear losing a fortune at our table."

"I shouldn't fear losing a fortune in any case. I never play cards for money. Even pennies," said Elizabeth firmly.

Mrs. Morrison looked rather taken aback at this remark. "Oh, my apologies. I did not realize you were a Methodist!"

Elizabeth laughed. "No offense taken, Mrs. Morrison. My abstinence from wagering has no religious roots, truly. I have just seen too many evil results from the practice to engage in it myself."

At this remark, a strained silence fell over the room. Voicing an opposition to gambling among the country gentry appeared to be akin to voicing support for Napoleon's return from St. Helena, Elizabeth thought acidly. Well, she had a right to her opinions, and she would not retract them simply because they offended her social superiors.

At this thought, she stopped. She could not keep saying whatever amused her. She owed much to the Rivertons and it was most unkind to be so churlish. Embarrassed, she lapsed into silence.

"If not cards, Lady Mary, could I interest you in a game of chess?" Spencer lifted his head from his book, breaking the tension in the room. The gamesters returned to their match, the discussion of wagering instantly forgotten.

"Thank you, Mr. Willoughby," she said, ridiculously pleased that he assumed she would be familiar with the game. She had enjoyed it ever since her brother had taught it to her years ago, although she rarely played now, her aunts having no interest in it. "But it is such a slow and serious game—it doesn't seem like your type of amusement."

"Believe it or not, I do have a slow and serious side. It often confuses people." Spencer gave a short laugh.

Elizabeth moved across the room to settle on the chair next to his. "Normally, I would be most pleased to take you up on your suggestion," she said. "But I fear my concentration is not the best this evening."

She lowered her voice so that the Morrisons could not hear. "I am worried about the meeting with your solicitor tomorrow. If he cannot resolve my affairs quickly, I may need to escape to another location. Victor will not stop

looking until he finds me, and his search will bring him
here eventually."

"Please do not concern yourself about the matter tonight. There is nothing to be done until the morning. It
does no good to borrow trouble in the meantime."
Spencer closed his book and laid it on a small Sheraton
table. Elizabeth glanced at the title: *Récherches physico-
chimique.*

"I did not know you read French," she said. "Although, now that I think on it, I suppose you were required to learn it in school."

"I do not read it particularly well," he replied with a
wry grin. "I have been struggling through one section
for the better part of the evening. But, although I know
there is an English translation, I have been unable to
obtain one, so I must make do."

"What is the book about?"

"It records the observations of two French researchers
who are investigating the effects of heat and light on
various elements. A very dry subject, I know, but one
that interests me a great deal."

Elizabeth found herself intrigued. A debonair aristocrat with a secret interest in science was a unique indi-
vidual, at least in her experience.

"And what have they discovered?"

"In general, they argue that heat and light have much
the same effect. But an English scientist, Humphrey
Davy, disputes that hypothesis. In fact, I recently finished
rereading his *Elements of Chemical Philosophy.* That is
why I have returned to the French book—to reassess the
observations and determine which theory is most cred-
ible."

"How fascinating!" Elizabeth exclaimed. "How did
you become interested in such an unusual field?"

"Years ago, I attended a meeting at the Royal Insti-
tution in London," Mr. Willoughby replied, his eyes

dancing with enthusiasm. "The topic of discussion was . . ." Suddenly, he stopped.

"Please continue, Mr. Willoughby," she encouraged him.

"Oh, Lady Mary, please forgive me for rattling on. I am sure this is of no interest to you."

"But it is!" she protested.

"But I had promised you a game of chess." He rose from his chair and Elizabeth sensed that, for some reason she did not understand, the scientific discussion was closed. At least for now.

Aware for the first time that their hushed conversation by the fire might appear odd to the Morrisons, she said in a loud voice, "Thank you for your offer of a game, Mr. Willoughby. I do believe some form of distraction is in order, although I truly doubt I have the presence of mind for chess. May I propose billiards as an alternative?"

Again, her remarks brought a hush over the room. "Billiards, Lady Mary?" Mrs. Morrison inquired sharply, breaking the silence. "Surely you do not play such a masculine game?"

Blast, Elizabeth thought. *I have put my foot in it once again.*

She was not at all used to having her statements and actions constantly questioned. At Roger Scott Importing, her word was law, despite the fact that she was a mere woman. If she had announced that she wanted to sing an aria in the courtyard of the Royal Exchange, not one employee would have dared contradict her. They might have thought her mad—indeed, she suspected that more than one of her employees considered a woman in business demented by definition—but they would have let her do as she wished.

But, as she was coming to learn, Linden Park was not her office. And if she was going to repay the Rivertons' generosity, she was going to have to try harder to adapt to her new milieu.

"My father taught me, after my brother passed away," she explained. "They used to play almost every night, and he sorely missed his partner."

"I would be more than pleased to test your mettle," said Spencer, saving her from embarrassment for the second time in a quarter hour. As she watched him rise from his chair and stroll across the room, an almost feline grace evident in every step, she wondered whether her concentration would be any better at billiards than it would have been at chess.

"Do you think it wise to play alone?" Lady Riverton asked in a hesitant voice.

"Oh no, Lady Riverton. I think Mr. Willoughby ought to bring along a footman for moral support. My father taught me well, and I firmly intend to win this match!" Elizabeth replied merrily.

She just might best me, Spencer thought as he missed a ridiculously easy shot. He watched as his cue ball rolled uselessly past the red ball to the center of the green felt.

"How unfortunate," Miss Scott remarked, as she moved to line up her shot, not sounding regretful in the slightest. "But it does put me at a distinct advantage."

He noticed that she splayed her long, slim fingers beneath the cue expertly, hooking one finger over the cue for stability. The few women he had played against in the past had used a simpler bridge, merely supporting the cue with a thumb. Miss Scott's technique was both more difficult to achieve and more effective.

Having prepared her shot, she leaned over the polished oak billiard table, cue poised elegantly behind her.

His game was inferior tonight. He was simply not used

to playing against a female opponent. Spencer forced himself to stare at the top of Miss Scott's head rather than at more intriguing places.

She banked the cue ball off the left cushion and into the red ball, sending the latter ricocheting into the nearest side pocket. As it rattled into the space, she laughed.

Good Lord, she had won. The game had passed so quickly he had barely been aware of it.

Watching his opponent straighten, Spencer couldn't help but notice the way her blue silk dress clung to her slim curves. Had the fashions changed this Season without his awareness? He could not recollect noticing any young women in London wearing a garment that was quite as fetching.

The gown was cut in a simple style, and yet Miss Scott looked more charming in it than would the most popular actress in Drury Lane. Despite himself, he let his gaze trace a path from the slightly disheveled chestnut curls at her nape to the line of tiny embroidered flowers that edged the neckline of her dress.

It was no mystery why his concentration was off.

"I believe that's the match," Miss Scott said, grinning as she leaned her cue against the wall. "May I challenge you to another?"

"I believe my male pride requires a rematch," Spencer replied. "If it ever gets out that a mere woman bested me in billiards, I shall never be able to hold up my head again in White's."

"Are you planning to go back to London soon?" she inquired, as she extracted the red ball and rolled it toward the top cushion.

"Unfortunately, yes. I will be leaving in a few days, once our solicitor has met with you. I have some business in the City early next week that I must attend to.

"I would much rather stay here until your affairs are settled, and I can be assured you can return to London

safely protected from Victor Newfield," he continued.
"But I know that Ben, my father, and the servants will
be on the watch."

She was most curious about the nature of his business
in London, but she did not want to pry. So instead, she
said, "It is most kind of you to be concerned for my
safety. But do not worry for an instant about going to
London. I will be well protected by your family here.
And, if we are lucky, everything will be settled quickly
and I shan't need to impose on your hospitality for long."

Spencer suppressed a wave of regret at her remarks,
but then caught himself up short. He could not afford to
develop a *tendre* for Elizabeth Scott. The way his fi-
nances were at the minute, he could barely afford a bottle
of port. He hadn't the blunt to entertain a woman in
style, particularly a woman of Miss Scott's evident
wealth.

And if he even tried, she would likely suspect he was
a fortune hunter, he reflected.

"It is your first shot, Mr. Willoughby," she said, breaking into his train of thought.

"Of course." He placed his cue ball in the D, leaned
over the table, and threaded the cue through the curve
of his index finger. He sighted the red ball along his
cue, lining up a shot into the bottom corner pocket. Cue-
ing cleanly, he knocked the red ball into the pocket with
a satisfying *thwack*.

He scored eleven points in quick succession, feeling
quite pleased with his success. As he was lining up a
somewhat tricky shot, Miss Scott came around the table
and peered around his right arm.

"That's going to be difficult," she observed, so close
that he could hear her breathing.

The shot suddenly seemed more difficult than he had
anticipated.

"I have done it several times before," he said with feigned casualness.

"I have no doubt. Do you practice much when you are here?"

He tried to concentrate more on the table, and less on her slim white wrist resting close to him on the edge of the table.

"Not a great deal. Neither my father nor Benjamin are terribly keen players." He drew back his cue, breathing in deeply. The faint aroma of rosewater filled his nostrils.

He miscued badly, sending his cue ball sailing straight past the red ball and into a side pocket.

"Perhaps you should practice more," she said, a wide grin taking any bite out of her words.

"Hoyden." He grinned back. "That puts me down three. Your shot, Miss Scott."

She placed her cue ball in the D. "So how do you normally fill your days here at Linden Park?" she asked.

"Oh, I help Benjamin when he will allow me to do so. Mainly, I catch up on my sleep and play the gentleman of leisure. Keep the occasional guests entertained in the evenings. That sort of thing passes the time quite admirably."

He was strangely reluctant to tell Miss Scott how he generally spent most of his days on the estate: holed up in his workroom. He had little stomach for another debate about the usefulness, or lack thereof, of his experiments. The conversation with Benjamin earlier in the day had been quite enough.

"Do you not get bored?"

"Not in the slightest. I am very easily amused," he said with his trademark insouciance.

Miss Scott gave him a strange glance he could not interpret. She said nothing, however, merely leaned over the table to make her first shot. She cued the ball with a bit too much force, sending it slamming into the red ball. The red ball bounced across the table, wide of the corner pocket for which she had obviously been aiming.

"I believe it is your turn, Mr. Willoughby," she said in a distant voice, moving away from the table to give him room to line up his shot.

He examined the table, wracking his brain to account for her sudden coolness. What had he said? What had he done? He was at a loss to account for the sudden drop in temperature in the room. Drawing back his cue, he miscued, sending his cue ball straight into a center pocket. It was going to be a long demmed game.

Later that night, Elizabeth sat before the gilt-edged mirror in her room, brushing out her hair. The more elaborate style she had adopted since arriving at Linden Park tended to leave her thick hair rather tangled by the end of the day.

Maisie, the young housemaid who had been assigned to serve as her abigail for the duration of her stay, had offered to take on the difficult job, but Elizabeth preferred to do such tasks herself. She had always enjoyed having time before bed to think quietly about the events of the day. At home, she had also used the pause to make a mental list of her tasks for the next morn: meetings to schedule, wholesalers to approach, accounts to review.

As her life at Linden Park involved few activities that required advance planning, however, she cast her mind back to the events of the evening just past. Despite herself, her thoughts turned immediately to Spencer Willoughby.

She had been enjoying their game of billiards a great deal, until he had remarked that his days were largely idle ones. The thought that he was yet another aimless member of the aristocracy, drifting through life with neither purpose nor ambition, had upset her so much that she had played poorly for the rest of the evening.

It should not have come as a surprise, she told herself as she removed a few of the many pins needed to keep her hair restrained in the complicated upsweep she now wore. Most members of his class were similarly unencumbered by responsibilities.

And yet, she had suspected there was much more to Spencer Willoughby. He did not give off the air of indolence so noticeable in the young bucks she sometimes observed lounging on street corners in London, whose main occupation appeared to be sizing up the attributes of female shoppers strolling by.

His interest in such an arcane subject as chemistry indicated a greater depth to his character than he seemed willing to reveal, Elizabeth thought as she brushed her hair with a silver-backed brush. The chestnut mass tumbled to her waist. Such a length of hair was most impractical in her line of work, as she was always leaning over boxes or tilting her head upward to gaze at ships, with the result that part of her coiffeur was always escaping from its pins. But her long hair was the one feminine vanity Elizabeth permitted herself.

I really am inordinately proud of it, she thought as she worked the last section loose. *It would behoove me to be more modest. Goodness knows, I am no beauty.*

Brushing out the final curl, then rising from the table, she suddenly wondered how Mr. Willoughby would react if he could see her hair thus undone. Perhaps it would cause him to think of her as more than a friend.

Perhaps he already thought of her in a different light. She remembered how he had miscued after she came to stand beside him.

She knew that she had been most aware of him as they stood side by side at the table. Elizabeth remembered being fascinated by his capable hands as he handled the cue, and inhaling the faint, spicy scent of sandalwood mixed with leather and wool that seemed to follow him everywhere.

Just because she had noticed him did not mean he had taken any notice of her. And even if he had, an easygoing aristocrat with his pockets to let was the last sort of person whose interest she should return.

As Elizabeth laid her dressing gown on a low bench and climbed into bed, she recalled Lady Riverton's allusion to some mysterious work Spencer did in the barn. Perhaps it was related to his interest in science?

But if he was conducting experiments in the barn, why would he pretend to be a man of leisure?

And what sort of business did he have in London? Was it related to chemistry, or was it of a more personal nature?

Her mind continuing to roil with such questions, Elizabeth fell into a fitful sleep.

"For the last time, you have not the slightest clue which one of these estates my dear cousin has hared off to? Or do you require some . . . assistance . . . to remember that information?" Victor Newfield pitched his voice low, and gave his large knuckles a long, luxurious crack. He was satisfied to see the color drain from Gerald Reynolds's round face.

"For the last time, I assure you that I do not know!" Reynolds huffed. "I told you everything the last time I was here. She is with a family called the Rivertons. I brought you the list of their estates. Beyond that, I know nothing. I did try, but the chit wouldn't tell me a thing with that blond toff hovering behind her," the older man finished sulkily.

"All right." Victor gave up. It appeared the idiot truly had shared all his knowledge, sparse though it was.

He stood up from his battered oak desk, crossed the untidy office of Newfield and Son, and picked up a scrap of foolscap covered with Reynolds's scrawling handwriting. "Aldcross Hall, West Grange, Linden Park, Liswich Manor," he read out. "Four estates in four parts of England. Where do you suggest I start?"

"The estates closest to London would be the most reasonable. If she is at one of them, you will find her quickly and save yourself a further trip." Reynolds puffed up, pleased with himself, despite the fact that it was so desperately obvious that a child could have come up with that.

"I had already jumped to that conclusion," Victor replied with a humorless laugh. "That means either Liswich Manor or Aldcross Hall. I suppose I shall try Aldcross Hall. I have a rough idea where it is, at least."

"I might be able to help." William Roberts, a young man of few words who sometimes did unpleasant errands for Victor, spoke up from the corner where he had been wordlessly observing the conversation.

"Yes?" Victor prompted him.

"M'sister lives not far from Linden Park," Will explained, strolling across the room and leaning against Victor's desk. "Married some deadly dull country squire. Perhaps she knows this Riverton crew. I could drop in on my beloved sib for an unexpected visit. Do a little nosing around."

"Excellent idea," Victor said.

"What does the woman look like?" Will asked. "Perhaps I shall find her hiding in some disused parlor, pretending to be the maid."

"Brown hair. Small. I believe her eyes are green. Attractive enough, I suppose, if one can overlook her personality." Victor stuffed the list of the Rivertons' estates into a small traveling bag. "If you find anything worth reporting, send a message to me at the Fox and Hound in Aldcross."

It occurred to him that he would need more money than he currently possessed if he was to spend an unknown amount of time staying at inns. "Reynolds, give me some blunt," he demanded crossly. "It is the least you can do, seeing as you let the bloody baggage go."

Wordlessly, Gerald Reynolds handed over his purse. Victor dumped the contents into his traveling bag and handed the empty purse back.

"Seems like an awful lot of trouble, though, to wander across half of England looking for some chit who doesn't want to be found," Will observed.

"It is no matter. It would be good for me to be away from Town for a few weeks at present, in any case. If I was not on this errand, I would need to make myself scarce some other way. I have had no word from that idiot, Henry Cox. I must assume that your encounter with him has not changed his mind regarding my debt."

Will bristled at the implied criticism. "The man was frightened. We saw to that."

"But he has not offered to cancel my debt, and I cannot run the risk that he will conquer his fears of retribution and have me arrested." Victor buckled the traveling bag. "I must get the money to pay him as soon as possible."

"But surely there must be some other way to pay your debts, Newfield, than by wedding Elizabeth Scott?" Will asked.

"If there were, I should have taken it long ago. Believe me, marrying that sour stick of a woman is my very last resort. All I want is her money. Once we are leg-shackled and her money is mine, she can burn in hell for all I care." Victor picked up his bag, strode across the room and yanked open the door.

Seven

The estate office at Linden Park was a small room at the back of the house. Tall bookshelves lined the walls, and a pair of windows shrouded in wine-colored velvet overlooked the kitchen garden. A small fire crackled in the grate, warding off the early morning chill.

Elizabeth still felt cold, however, as she examined the sheaf of papers the Rivertons' solicitor, Mr. Mason, had laid before her for her perusal. The amount of work needed to shield her financial affairs from Victor's prying fingers appeared to be immense.

"It is somewhat unusual for a wife to separate her property from her husband's control," Mr. Mason was saying. "In fact, under common law, it is impossible to do so."

"It is obvious, then, that women have had no hand in shaping common law," Elizabeth remarked tartly. "I am certain I am not the first woman in England to wish to retain a few pence in her own name."

"If wishes were horses, beggars would ride," replied the lawyer. "Many women may wish for such a thing, but the common law is the law. Fortunately, you are a woman of some means. As a result, under the parallel law system known as equity, there are mechanisms available to help you. It will, however, take time to set up a trust that can adequately protect your extensive assets."

"So it appears. But is there no way to do things

quickly for the interim, and resolve the remaining issues later? It is very difficult for me to be absent from my business for even a few days. An absence of a few *weeks* is almost inconceivable." Elizabeth tried, and failed, to keep the impatience from her voice.

Theodore Mason sighed, spreading his gold-ringed fingers across his ample waistcoat. "I wish there were a quicker way. But, aside from everything else, we must wait until your friend Mr. Baker gives his assent to becoming your trustee. And then, once the papers are drawn up, it will take time to convey them back and forth to Yorkshire."

She nodded.

"And I am afraid I am also trapped by the requirements of the law," Mr. Mason went on. "If you were to return to London before everything was watertight, and found yourself ensnared by Mr. Newfield, all our work would be for naught. Take the time to do things correctly from the beginning, Miss Scott, and you shall not regret it later."

Elizabeth smiled. Despite everything, she still took pleasure in hearing her own name again, in being plain Miss Scott. It was a tiny bit of her old existence to cling to in this unfamiliar world in which she found herself.

"Well, I suppose if it must take several weeks, it must," she said. "I cannot like it, but I suppose I must live with it."

"I suppose you must, miss," said Mr. Mason with a patronizing little smile. Elizabeth gritted her teeth. After years of working in a man's world, she thought, her teeth were worn down to the nerves, so used was she to grinding them in the face of various males' notions of their own superiority. You would think she would have accepted it by now.

"I know it is most frustrating, Miss Scott, but Mr.

Mason is right," Mr. Willoughby piped up. "The documents must be perfect if you are to be completely safe."

Elizabeth nodded. "As I understand it, the trust must include four types of property: real property, personal property, chattels real, and chattels incorporeal." She tested the unfamiliar terms on her tongue. They sounded like diseases. "Am I correct?"

The lawyer murmured his assent.

"In other words, the land I own, my personal and business effects, the land I hold by lease, and the contracts and shares I own."

Mr. Mason smiled, a tepid expression Elizabeth sensed he did not have occasion to produce often. "You have a remarkably clear grasp of the intricacies of property law, Miss Scott, particularly for a female."

Elizabeth felt a curt reply springing to her lips. But before she could speak, Spencer Willoughby rose from his chair next to the lawyer and began to pace before the fire.

"Now, let us review," he began, sending her a commiserating look. She knew at once that he understood her fury at being patronized and was going to do his best to keep her from lashing out at the solicitor. He was right, of course. She could not afford to offend Mr. Mason. His work was crucial to protecting her estate from Victor.

Elizabeth gave a slight nod to Mr. Willoughby. He smiled back, then returned his attention to the solicitor.

"We have begun proceedings to protect Miss Scott's house, the Roger Scott Importing warehouse, the offices, the inventory, the company stock Miss Scott holds, the bank assets, and the company ships." He ticked off each item on his long fingers. "And the trust must also include the household contents, Miss Scott's clothing and jewelry, and the warehouses in Jamaica, correct?"

Mr. Mason nodded, scribbling a few notes on a piece of Linden Park stationery.

As Spencer continued to list the items to be covered, Elizabeth allowed herself a minute to simply contemplate him as he worked. He was a complete puzzle to her, she had to admit. A self-confessed man of leisure, fond of wit and fine clothes, gaming and wine, he yet had an undeniable air of authority when he chose to exercise it. He claimed to have no ambition in life, but he seemed to disappear for hours at a time during the day, engaged in his mysterious activities in the barn, she assumed. And he had once tried to become a soldier and a priest, even if he had later acquiesced to his family's wishes and given up those dreams.

She could not shake the feeling that there was more to Spencer Willoughby than the average highborn roué. She just wished she could put her finger on what that "more" was.

Giving up that train of thought, she returned her concentration to the conversation at hand. "Is there anything else you need me to do at the minute, Mr. Mason?" she inquired in her best professional voice, which she had perfected as a teenager to wield authority over clerks and stevedores twice her size and age.

"No, Miss Scott, I believe I have everything I need." The portly lawyer rose from his wing chair and gathered up his papers. "I shall be in contact with you in the next few days to give you an update on your affairs. In the meantime, I would counsel patience, m'dear."

Patience. Patience! She would love to see how patient Mr. Mason would be if he was afraid some loathsome relative was going to bundle him off into a forced marriage and take away his independence and everything his family had worked for.

Knowing she had to be polite to the officious solicitor, as his efforts were the best hope she had of evading

Victor at the minute, she pasted what she hoped resembled a sincere smile on her face. "I shall attempt to be patient," she said in crisp, formal tones. "Thank you so much for your assistance."

When the solicitor had departed in the company of a footman, Elizabeth drew in a long, deep breath. She suddenly felt extremely tired.

"He may not be the most charming solicitor in England, but he is very good at his work," Mr. Willoughby remarked, dropping back into his chair.

As always, she admired the easy grace with which he moved. He managed to make the simple act of sitting down almost like a movement in a dance.

Suddenly, she realized that the footman's departure, in order to escort Mr. Mason out, had left her alone for the moment with Mr. Willoughby. She should leave. It was improper to be here.

Do not be a green goose, she thought. She had been alone with men before, in the course of business. It was not as though she was a young miss fresh from the schoolroom, or indeed the sort of woman a man would consider compromising.

Why had the thought of compromise rarely occurred to her before, in the course of her business meetings with a wide variety of gentlemen?

Unwilling to ponder the answer to that question, she forced herself to respond to Mr. Willoughby's comment on the solicitor's abrasive manner.

"Was it that obvious that he grated on my nerves?" she asked.

"Not, perhaps, to most people. But I believe I have learned to read you rather well, Miss Scott. I have grown to fear the moments when your mouth folds into a thin line." He grinned.

Despite her embarrassment, Elizabeth smiled too. "I must admit, above all things, I detest being patronized."

"In that, I must sympathize with you."

Elizabeth, suddenly remembering his mother's dismissive remarks about Spencer in the carriage on the way to Linden Park, simply nodded.

"But let us forget about the pompous Mr. Mason for the time being. There is one thing that has been preying on my mind now for several days." He paused. Elizabeth tilted her head.

He took a deep breath and plunged ahead. "I hesitate to bring this up, as I do not want to agitate you, but I must know. Is Mr. Newfield likely to be dangerous?"

"Dangerous?" Elizabeth considered the idea. "Well, he is most dangerous in the sense that he wishes me to marry against my wishes."

"Forgive me, Miss Scott. I should have expressed myself more clearly." Mr. Willoughby paused. "I meant to determine whether Mr. Newfield is likely to be violent."

Elizabeth's heart began to thud against her breastbone, like a frightened bird attempting to escape a cage. Would Victor dare to do her physical harm? Or, worse, would he hurt her aunts . . . or Mr. Willoughby's family?

She forced herself to answer his question in a slow, calm voice.

"I must admit, I never used to consider him to be capable of violence. Victor is, at heart, a coward. But he has become increasingly desperate in the last months. When he seized me from the street in London last week, I did wonder fleetingly whether he meant me harm. But he did not strike me, nor do I believe he had a weapon."

"But he is desperate?"

"Oh yes, more than desperate. I suspect that I am the last thing that stands between him and debtors' prison. Above all else, Victor fears embarrassment. Fleet Prison would be his idea of Dante's Inferno."

"In that case, I will confess that I am rather relieved that Mr. Mason convinced you of the necessity of staying here until your affairs are completely in order. If you are at Linden Park, we can all keep watch over you. I should hate to think that you were in any physical danger whatsoever."

Despite herself, despite her misgivings about Mr. Willoughby's character, Elizabeth felt a warm flush of pleasure suffuse her cheeks. It had been a long time since anyone had voiced concern for her welfare. Her aunts, dear souls though they were, believed Elizabeth to be invincible. They assumed that since she could run a business, she could handle anyone and any situation by herself. They also had no idea of the true threat that Victor posed—Elizabeth had warned them that Victor had been trying to "court" her, and she had asked them to deny him entry to the house, but she had been careful to shelter them as far as possible from her deepest fears. As a result, they had only been mildly concerned for her safety over the past few weeks.

And, aside from her aunts, Elizabeth was largely alone in the world. Having someone else who cared about her—even in an impersonal way—was cheering. And the fact that that person was the kind but puzzling Mr. Willoughby was doubly so.

A scratch at the estate office door interrupted her thoughts. At Mr. Willoughby's response, a young footman entered. "Mrs. Timms and Miss Johnson have arrived, Lady Mary. They are waiting in the front drawing room."

Elizabeth rose quickly from her seat. "What lovely news! I did not expect to see my aunts until much later today."

"We shall be along presently," Mr. Willoughby told the footman, who nodded and withdrew.

"Mr. Willoughby, I must thank you again for your kindness in bringing my aunts to Linden Park," Elizabeth said as she gathered up some papers Mr. Mason had left behind for her to review. "It puts my mind somewhat at rest to have them here."

"It was my pleasure, Miss Scott, truly," he said, with a warm smile that did strange things to her heartbeat. Bending swiftly over the papers again, she hoped he could not see the faint flush she could feel staining her cheeks.

"Really, Elizabeth, are you certain you have not mis-read your cousin? He was never the most charming boy, that's true—took after his rackety father that way, I always thought, and I often told his mother so—but I cannot believe he would stoop to such depths. Kidnapping and forced marriage! Honestly, it seems unworthy of him. These little cakes are delightful, by the way." Louisa Timms paused for breath and plucked another pastry from a gold-rimmed platter on the low table before her.

"Louisa, try not to be a silly hen. Of course Elizabeth is telling the truth. Victor was always a bad seed, and I don't doubt that he could turn vicious in the right cir-cumstances." Harriet Johnson, as spare as her sister was plump, sipped delicately at her cup of clear tea, unsullied as always by milk, sugar, or lemon.

"But the gel has to marry someone sometime. Why not Victor? At least we know his people, where he comes from." Louisa bit mulishly into her cake.

"Why must she marry someone?"

"Now, Harriet, who is being foolish? It is the done thing."

Harriet set down her cup with a clatter. "I did not do so, and I have fared perfectly well. And your great love match with Archibald Timms did not exactly change your world for the better, you have to admit."

"My Archie was a good man," Louisa muttered, in a

tone that revealed that the two sisters had covered this ground many, many times before.

"A good man who promptly ran through your marriage portion and died, leaving you precisely back where you started. Really, Louisa, if Mary hadn't married Roger Scott, who actually made something of himself, we would both be out on the street or working as elderly nursemaids to heaven knows whom, and well you know it."

"Auntie Louisa," Elizabeth interjected somewhat desperately. She was well used to their constant nattering, but she could see that Lady Riverton and Mr. Willoughby were somewhat aghast, presuming that a full-scale family row was in progress. She did not know how to explain that such conversations were the warp and weft of her aunts' existence. The two women had long since stopped communicating in any other way, and neither took the other's words at all seriously. In fact, the elderly pair were devoted to each other, despite outward appearances.

"Auntie Louisa," she said again, this time succeeding in distracting her aunt from a plate of ginger biscuits a young maid had just placed on the table. "You are so good-hearted that I know you cannot believe such dreadful things about Victor. But they are true, I assure you. And I can also assure you that I have no intention of marrying him."

Even if Victor might have thought she did. It might have been wrong to mislead him, but it was too late to wallow in regrets now.

"I can survive very well alone," Elizabeth added. "I have made my own way so far, and I do not need a man to provide for me, fortunately."

"Well said, Lady Mary," said Mr. Willoughby from the other side of the room, an enigmatic expression on his handsome face.

"Oh yes, that's right. I had quite forgotten. We must

call you Lady Mary now!" Aunt Louisa tittered, the debate over marriage forgotten. "My goodness, one of the
Quality, are we? Ready for our presentation at Court?"

Elizabeth groaned inwardly. Trust sweet, dotty Aunt
Louisa to say something awkward in front of their kind
hosts.

As usual, Mr. Willoughby stepped in to smooth things
over before any feathers could be ruffled. "Never could
stand Court, myself," he said with a grin. "Too many
toffs standing around in ridiculous costumes. If I want
to see that, I prefer to go to the theater. The dialogue
and the drink are both better."

As everyone in the room laughed, Lady Riverton
piped up from the low Grecian sofa where she had settled
herself to pour the tea. "Speaking of ridiculous costumes, Spencer, I have been thinking that we should host
a small ball to welcome Mrs. Timms and Miss Johnson
to the neighborhood."

At this suggestion, Aunt Louisa smiled widely and
smoothed down her voluminous silk traveling dress, as
though expecting a young man to approach that minute
and ask her to participate in a quadrille.

"Mother, I do not think it wise. Our guests are here
as part of an attempt to stay out of sight. Drawing attention to them would seem to be the last thing we should
do."

Lady Riverton sighed. "I suppose you are right,
Spencer, although it does seem like a dreadful *faux pas*
to have guests and not welcome them properly. I feel
remiss that we have done nothing more for Lady Mary
than invite the Morrisons over for cards." She paused,
tapping her fingers against the lid of the Wedgwood tea-
pot. "I know! We shall have a dinner party. Just a small
one," she added hastily, as Mr. Willoughby's brows drew
together. "A few people we have known forever. Nothing

more, I promise." She gave her youngest son a pleading smile.

"A few?" He raised his eyebrows. "Please define 'few.' I have known some of your 'small gatherings' to be quite substantial crushes."

Lady Riverton gazed up toward the ceiling, as though writing a guest list in the air. "Oh, let me see. Perhaps forty?"

"Forty!" Mr. Willoughby barked. "No, that number is far too dangerous."

"But anything smaller will look inhospitable," Lady Riverton complained.

Her son kept silent but gave her an implacable look.

"Well, if we must be so secretive about things, I suppose I could limit it to thirty."

"A dozen." Mr. Willoughby's voice was firm, and Elizabeth felt a warm glow of admiration for him. Despite her substantial negotiating skills, she was not at all certain she could have bested Lady Riverton when that lady was in a determined frame of mind.

Mr. Willoughby's mother sighed. "Well, I suppose a modest party will require less effort to coordinate. Are you certain that it shall pose no harm to Miss Scott and her family?"

Mr. Willoughby shook his fair head. "I am not positive, but I do hate to spoil your fun, Mother. I don't suppose a small supper shall cause any harm. If you ladies would enjoy it, that is?" he asked Elizabeth's aunts.

"Enjoy it? We should be most pleased to attend!" Aunt Louisa cried.

"Yes, indeed, it is very thoughtful of you," Aunt Harriet said in the gruff voice that Elizabeth knew meant her taciturn aunt was touched.

How generous the Rivertons were, to be so considerate of the comfort of two strangers. It had been a long time since she had seen her aunts as excited about a social event.

"It is settled then," Lady Riverton said, rising from the table and rubbing her hands together. "If you will excuse me, ladies, Spencer, I must meet with Cook immediately to discuss menus." She bustled away in a flurry of silken skirts.

Mr. Willoughby caught Elizabeth's eye over the gray heads of the two older ladies and grinned. Elizabeth smiled back, pleased to be included in his private amusement.

Eight

Waterford crystal, delicate china, and heavy Sheffield plate glittered in the candlelight as the footmen brought in the main course.

Spencer glanced down the long, linen-swathed table at Miss Scott's elderly relatives. Louisa Timms was in fine form, chattering to Mrs. Morrison and her daughter. The daughter, a pretty but insipid girl named Annabel, giggled almost incessantly at a tale Louisa was telling. He remembered how much girlish giggling had always annoyed him.

Miss Scott never giggled.

Resolutely pushing that thought away, he turned his attention to Harriet Johnson. She had dispensed with her usual austere garb for the evening, choosing a cranberry velvet that warmed her normally pallid complexion. Like her sister, she was deeply engaged in conversation, in this case with Benjamin.

Well, perhaps interrogation would be a better description of their exchange than conversation, Spencer amended with an inward grin. Miss Johnson appeared to be drilling Ben with a series of questions, punctuating them with imperious raps on the table—probably when his brother was answering in his characteristic drawl. But as both were smiling, all seemed to be in order.

He was pleased to see that the older ladies were enjoying the dinner party his mother had arranged. Miss

Scott had been most worried that they might be shy and
hesitant in the company of so many strangers. She had
also worried that they would not be able to adapt to their
new identities—as Lady Henrietta and Lady Louisa
Dixon. Harriet had accepted a new Christian name with
alacrity, but Louisa had staunchly declared that she herself would never remember to answer to anything but
Louisa. Despite this minor hurdle, the aunts appeared to
be taking their elevation in status with perfect ease.

"Louisa! For heaven's sake, get to the point of the
story before Mrs. Morrison expires due to protracted
confusion," Miss Johnson exclaimed. Distracted from her
inquisition of Ben by a burst of laughter from her sister,
she had temporarily turned her attention to Mrs. Timms.

Yes, indeed, Miss Scott's aunts seemed most relaxed
in their new roles, Spencer thought. Their manner toward
each other had not altered one whit.

As though he couldn't help himself, he turned his gaze
from his older houseguests and looked once more to
Miss Scott. He had not been able to take his eyes from
her for most of the evening, no matter how often he
reminded himself that he was in no position to pursue
an amorous liaison, especially one with a young woman
who proclaimed she had no interest in and little use for
men.

Perhaps it was the dress. Tonight, she was wearing an
evening gown of rich purple silk that left her arms completely bare. Around her long throat was a circlet of
pearls. The necklace drew his attention to the fact that
the gown was cut much lower than Miss Scott's usual
demure day dresses, thus revealing a tantalizing expanse
of creamy white skin. Really, was there some shortage
of fabric in England that had given rise to this sudden
onslaught of devilish fashions?

Or perhaps the reason for his interest in Miss Scott
tonight was the fact that she had been deep in conver-

sation for the last twenty minutes with a rather rakish-looking young man whom Spencer had never met before this evening. William Roberts had come along with his sister, Mrs. Campbell, a longtime neighbor Lady Riverton had encountered in town several days ago and had impulsively invited. The London man was a tradesman, a fact that at first had given Spencer great worry. He had watched carefully as Roberts was introduced to Miss Scott, but she had not shown the slightest flicker of recognition. Roberts, for his part, had bowed politely, his face devoid of any expression save polite interest.

Despite his profession, William Roberts was dressed in the highest stare of fashion. Perhaps too high, Spencer thought sourly, noting the younger man's bright blue waistcoat and impossibly high shirt points. He was surprised Roberts had not done himself grave injury with the ridiculous things.

My, aren't we being facetious tonight? he mocked himself. It wasn't in his character to poke fun at others; he usually reserved his choicest barbs for himself. But he didn't like the look of Mr. Roberts, although if pressed, he would not be able to give one reason for his unease. Aside from the fact that he was jealous of the man's monopoly of Elizabeth Scott.

Behave yourself, he thought. Just because he had no hope of winning Miss Scott's affections did not mean she should never look at another.

His admonitions did no good. Something about Mr. Roberts's manner bothered him—something aside from mere jealousy. His fascination with Miss Scott, to the exclusion of other guests seated nearby, seemed a little too intense.

"Would you like another glass of wine, Mr. Willoughby?" inquired a voice at his elbow. Mrs. Campbell was proffering the bottle of hock. Judging by her flushed face and merry voice, she had already partaken well of it herself.

"Yes, thank you," he said absently, holding out his glass while continuing to stare at the couple across the table.

"It does seem they are getting along very well, does it not?" Mrs. Campbell observed.

"Do you think so?" he asked, a bit more sharply than he had intended.

"Indeed. Lady Mary is a lovely young woman. And our Will is more than her match, for all that he is a mere tradesman."

Spencer forced himself to focus on Mrs. Campbell's comments, lest he give Mrs. Campbell the impression that he was a snob. It wasn't that he thought Mr. Roberts was not good enough for Miss Scott. It was that he thought *no one* was a good enough match for her.

"No, your brother is a fine man," he hastened to reassure Mrs. Campbell, even as he tried to pinpoint what it was about the mysterious Mr. Roberts that made him uncomfortable. "I am glad he could attend our soiree."

"Thank you so much for inviting us," Mrs. Campbell replied, evidently mollified. "I was at a bit of a loss as to how to amuse Will when he arrived unexpectedly. He rarely ventures far from London, and I feared he would be bored with our small, provincial existence."

She continued to converse in this vein, occasionally drawing her stolid husband into the discussion, to which he added well-practiced grunts and nods. Spencer, following his lead, nodded and murmured when it seemed to be required, but continued to keep one eye on the couple across the table.

"And how long have you been in Staffordshire?" he heard the younger man ask. He strained his ears to hear Miss Scott's murmured reply, but could not.

A few minutes later, in between Mrs. Campbell's ramblings, he heard her brother ask Miss Scott, "And do you visit the Rivertons often?"

Several minutes later, Mr. Roberts asked, "How long do you intend to stay at Linden Park?"

He certainly seemed an inquisitive sort, Spencer noted. But then, so was Miss Johnson, and she posed no threat to anyone.

However, William Roberts was from London, and a tradesman.

"What line of business are you involved in, Mr. Roberts?" Spencer raised his voice slightly to be heard across the noisy table.

"Various retail enterprises," his guest replied. "Dry goods, foodstuffs. Anything to earn a few pence."

Spencer kept his face neutral. He disliked the man's vagueness. In his experience, most businesspeople loved nothing better than talking about their commercial activities.

But there was always an exception to every rule. He must not let his concern for Miss Scott's welfare make him unduly suspicious of every stranger he met.

He did, however, keep one ear cocked toward the conversation across the table, even as he continued nodding politely to Mrs. Campbell. Her verbosity was a blessing, he thought. At least it relieved him of the necessity of keeping up his end of the conversation.

"And are you enjoying your stay in the country, Lady Mary?" Will Roberts asked.

"Very much. It is a lovely property."

"How do you amuse yourself each day?"

Miss Scott gave an odd little smile. "Oh, I write letters, go for walks, engage in the odd bit of . . . needlework. All the usual country occupations, and nothing too taxing."

Spencer was amused. He had never seen her set one

stitch to a sampler, and he could not imagine anything less likely to keep her occupied.

"Ah, yes, it must be wonderful, to live a life of leisure," Mr. Roberts murmured. "I would be most pleased not to be forced to engage in 'getting and spending,' as some poet or other so succinctly phrased it. But someone, I suppose, must keep the economy afloat."

"Everyone, at every station, does his part," Miss Scott replied with a slight touch of reproof in her voice, much to Spencer's surprise. For someone who seemed so convinced that the aristocracy was lazy, she was very quick to spring to its defense. Or perhaps that was just part of her Lady Mary persona.

"That's true," Spencer chipped in without thinking, quick to reinforce any positive thoughts Miss Scott harbored toward his class. "Why, even I work on a few worthwhile projects myself, in my copious free time."

"I had noticed that you do disappear for hours at a stretch," Miss Scott remarked, turning luminous green eyes toward him. He noticed, for the first time, that they were not a uniform green. Instead, her pale green irises were flecked with gold and rimmed in a deeper, almost emerald color.

"Yes," he put in quickly, realizing he had been staring. "I have my interests."

"What would those be?" Her amazing eyes continued to bore into his. "Would they be related to your study of the properties of elements?"

Ah, he was trapped now, he realized. Knowing Miss Scott as he already did, he suspected she would pursue this line of questioning until she had an answer that satisfied her curiosity.

He was loath, however, to expose himself to her scorn. He also didn't want to extend the discussion of his research to a point where all the guests at the table would hear it and feel compelled to offer their opinions.

He glanced at Mr. Roberts, but that gentleman was responding to something Miss Morrison, seated on his right, had asked him.

"Oh, just a small hobby. Really, it is not important."

"It is important to *me*, Mr. Willoughby," she replied. "You know so much about me, and yet I know so little about you. Please tell me more. It is only courteous." Her smile was both gentle and mischievous.

She had a point. It was churlish to be so secretive. And she did appear to have a genuine curiosity.

"I do a little scientific research," Spencer conceded.

"Really!" Her eyes lit up. "So I had come to suspect. In the area of heat and light?"

"Light, mainly. And optics."

"How fascinating! And where do you carry out your work?" She rested her small chin on her intertwined hands and leaned across the table toward him.

"I have claimed a small corner of the barn for my workshop." He was surprised how pleasant it was to have someone show any interest at all in his work. The fact that Miss Scott was the intrigued party made it particularly pleasing.

"If you like, I could show you my work some day soon. I am engaged elsewhere tomorrow and the next day, but perhaps after that?" He forced a diffidence he did not feel into his voice. In reality, he found himself surprisingly eager for Miss Scott to see his work, despite the fact that she might scoff at his efforts. Somehow, though, as he regarded her sincere expression, he anticipated that she would not laugh.

"I would enjoy that very much," she murmured. "Very much indeed."

"And now here is the pudding!" Lady Riverton exclaimed from the other end of the table, as a footman brought in dessert. With relief, Spencer noticed that the promise of sweets had diverted the company's attention, making it unlikely that anyone would be tempted to pay any attention to his discussion with Miss Scott.

As the footmen finished preparing the drawing room for a round of country dances, pushing the long, heavy settle against the wall and rolling back a blue Aubusson rug, Miss Scott glanced across the room at Mr. Willoughby. For such a slight man, she thought, he had remarkable presence. There was something about the way he carried himself, the cut of his clothes, and the solicitous way he ensured that Aunt Louisa had the most comfortable chair in the room. Something that commanded respect.

His family's prominence and lineage probably had something to do with it as well, she reflected. The Riverton title extended back more than four hundred years, Lady Riverton had explained the other day as she told Elizabeth the story of some of the family portraits hanging in the drawing room. The first marquess had received his title during the Hundred Years' War for services rendered the king.

She reminded herself of this as she continued to watch Spencer Willoughby move with ease around the busy room. No matter how appealing he might be, he would never be interested in the likes of her. Not only was she a cit, but she was also an illegitimate one. All highborn men, even fourth sons, had to think about bloodlines and lineage. And although part of her heritage was just as blue-blooded as his, her birth on the wrong side of the marriage blanket made that point rather moot.

What on earth was she thinking? she chided herself. She had no business even daydreaming about romance. Once Mr. Mason finished wrapping up her legal affairs, she had to return to London and pick up the reins of the business. The business was her legacy, and she wasn't about to give it up for any man. Especially a man like Spencer Willoughby who—charming, handsome, and intelligent though he was—appeared to be a gambler.

Victor, while not exactly the smartest man she had ever met, was no fool, she reminded herself. And yet he had allowed his fondness for the gaming table to bring him to the brink of ruin.

And yet, she suspected that Mr. Willoughby was made of sterner stuff than Victor. Surely the occasional game of cards at White's was not tantamount to moral failure?

Stop it! she admonished herself. Men, and particularly blue bloods, were not for her.

No matter how attractive they were.

"I hope you will have fun this evening," Lady Riverton said somewhat anxiously. "We have no ballroom here at Linden Park, and our country amusements, I fear, are rather tame and provincial in comparison to the glitter of London."

Elizabeth gave her hostess a conspiratorial smile. "As you know, Lady Riverton, I am not much used to the London social scene," she said in a low voice. "This party has already been much more festive and elegant than my usual evening meal with Aunt Louisa and Aunt Harriet. And I'm afraid my dancing skills are somewhat rusty."

"Oh, my dear, do not trouble yourself about such things. We are none of us tremendously skilled in that area!" her hostess said with a musical little laugh.

Elizabeth was skeptical. She suspected that Lady Riverton and her sons were more than competent dancers.

As if reading her thoughts, the youngest Mr. Willoughby materialized at her elbow. "Lady Mary, I believe the festivities are about to begin. May I request the first dance?"

Despite all her earlier admonitions to herself, she

could feel a flush of pleasure suffusing her cheeks at his offer. "Thank you, Mr. Willoughby. I would be delighted."

He grinned as he escorted her toward the area that had been cleared for dancing. Her face grew warmer, until she wondered whether others would remark on it. She must be almost scarlet.

They took their places opposite each other in two lines that soon included Lady Riverton and Mr. Roberts, young Annabel Morrison and Benjamin Willoughby, and a reluctant-looking Lord Riverton and Mrs. Morrison. Elizabeth hoped she did not look as ridiculously excited as she felt.

To her surprise, she saw Aunt Harriet settle down at the pianoforte to begin the first piece.

"Why, Aunt Henrietta! I have not seen you play in years," she exclaimed.

"Oh, I do practice occasionally. It is just that you seldom see me." Her aunt smiled.

Because I am usually at the office, Elizabeth though with a slight pang.

There was no time to think further about the matter, however, as Aunt Harriet launched into a sprightly reel.

Lord Riverton and Mrs. Morrison were the top couple, and Elizabeth tried to watch their steps with great concentration. It had been a long time since she had had the occasion to dance, and the intricate combination of figures seemed much more complicated than she remembered.

Her concentration was not as complete as it could have been, however, as Mr. Willoughby's light touch on her elbow was rather distracting.

In what seemed like an instant, her host and Mrs. Morrison had finished and retired to the end of the line. Lady Riverton and Mr. Roberts were now top couple, which meant that she and Mr. Willoughby were second and would shortly be required to move. A small knot of panic formed in her stomach. How embarrassing it would be to be shown up as an awkward cit in this elegant company!

Mr. Willoughby held out his hand to her, and she slid hers into it. His grasp was strong and assured, and her fingers began to tingle as if she had suddenly immersed them in a warm, comforting bath.

She moved forward into the first steps she could recall. Suddenly nervous, she stared at her feet, as though she could will them into the right position.

"It is easier to dance if you look at your partner." Mr. Willoughby's voice was laced with kind humor.

Elizabeth raised her gaze to his vivid blue eyes. "My apologies, Mr. Willoughby. It is just that it has been many years since I have done this."

He smiled broadly, and the warmth flooded her body once again. Good heavens, he was devastating. How had he remained a bachelor for so long?

"I shall give you some quick instruction, then, Lady Mary. You are to exchange places with my mother now. Then you will dance a half turn with Mr. Roberts, then exchange places again and return to me."

He released her hand and she followed his instructions. As she placed her hand in Mr. Roberts's, that gentleman smiled at her in a distracted manner.

His hand felt like a cold fish in hers.

Within moments, she had returned to Mr. Willoughby's side. Observing Lady Riverton extending her hands to Mr. Roberts, Elizabeth clasped Mr. Willoughby's hand in both of hers, as he slid a strong arm about her waist.

"Next, we shall turn about, until we are facing Mr. Roberts and my mother, on the opposite side of the floor."

She did as he said, and managed not to trip over her

own feet. It was, she felt, a heroic accomplishment, as she seemed unable to focus on anything but the sensation of Mr. Willoughby's hand on the small of her back. That, and the exotic yet increasingly familiar scent of sandalwood that teased her nostrils when she leaned toward him.

Mr. Willoughby whispered, "Now we cross back to our original positions."

As she moved through the set, she gradually remembered the steps she had learned years ago, before Tony died, when she was merely the daughter of the Scott family and not its scion.

The third set, when she and Mr. Willoughby were top couple, was somewhat easier, thanks in large part to her partner's graceful, confident lead. At the end of the set, as they retired to the end of the line, he remarked, "You did marvelously, Lady Mary. One would never know you were the least bit unpracticed."

Despite the fact that she knew he was being kind, she glowed with pleasure. The man had charm to spare. "With your assistance, it was not that difficult," she whispered back. "Thank you so much, Mr. Willoughby."

As the dance came to an end, and she curtsied to Mr. Willoughby, the inquisitive Mr. Roberts approached to request the next dance. Elizabeth suppressed a tiny sigh. She supposed it would not do to dance each set with Mr. Willoughby, although he was such a charming and easy companion that the notion was tempting.

Mr. Roberts, on the other hand, seemed a bit too interested in Elizabeth's life for her comfort. She supposed he was just making an effort to be sociable, and that she should do the same.

"Lady Mary," he said formally, holding out his hand to her.

As they moved through the set, she realized he was

even more inept at dancing than she. Well, she supposed, we cits are probably equally unskilled in the fine arts.

"So how are you related to Lady Riverton?" he asked as they executed a half promenade.

"She and my mother were cousins," she replied, hoping she had remembered that part of her story correctly.

"And your aunts?"

"They are my father's sisters." My goodness, this business of maintaining a different identity was difficult. She decided to put a halt to Mr. Roberts's questioning, at least temporarily.

"And you, Mr. Roberts? Is Mrs. Campbell your only sister?"

"Oh no, I have five others."

"Five! How marvelous. I would have loved to have had five sisters."

"You are an only child, then?"

How on earth had the conversation come so quickly back to her?

"No, I . . . have . . . two brothers," she improvised, wishing desperately for the set to end. This was not nearly as enjoyable as dancing with Mr. Willoughby, and not only because Mr. Roberts did not have the blond man's easy grace.

His relentless questions made her most uneasy. From beneath lowered lashes, she assessed him, trying to ascertain whether she had ever encountered him in London. Not a spark of recognition flared in her mind.

Perhaps he is simply ill-bred, she thought. Or just curious. She recalled Lady Riverton's stream of questions in the carriage, and remembered seeing Aunt Harriet interrogating poor Benjamin Willoughby at the dinner table. Perhaps everyone was more avid to hear the stories of others than Elizabeth herself was.

Although she was most curious to hear more of Spencer Willoughby's history.

She puffed out her breath impatiently. She must stop allowing her thoughts to move in that gentleman's direction. With fresh resolve, she turned toward her partner and favored him with a bright smile.

Finally, Aunt Harriet finished her second piece with a flourish. Gratefully, Elizabeth took her leave of her nosy partner and sank into a comfortable wing chair pressed against the wall. Dancing was most exhausting work.

"May I have the honor of this next dance?" asked Benjamin Willoughby, with the shy smile that was so like his brother's, and yet so different.

"Thank you, Mr. Willoughby, but I am afraid I am a bit fatigued." Elizabeth smiled. In truth, she wanted to avoid another encounter with Mr. Roberts on the dance floor—however brief—until she had finished reviewing her improvised biography.

"I sympathize, Lady Mary," Annabel Morrison said as she dropped into the chair next to Elizabeth's. "That set quite did me in!"

Benjamin Willoughby gave them both a friendly smile and departed in search of another partner.

As the next set began, Elizabeth found her gaze drawn to the younger Mr. Willoughby, partnered this time with Mrs. Campbell. As always, he looked remarkably well turned out for a man of empty pockets. His coat of forest green superfine was exquisitely tailored to his slim shoulders, and his black pantaloons fit like a second skin. In a room full of gentlemen, some much older and more distinguished than he, Spencer Willoughby cut by far the most elegant swath.

"The youngest Mr. Willoughby has always been the most popular of the brothers here at Linden Park," Annabel Morrison said in a confidential voice. Startled, Elizabeth glanced at the younger girl and saw she had been following Elizabeth's gaze.

Really, Elizabeth admonished herself, *if I cannot stop myself from mooning over Spencer Willoughby, I must at least refrain from being so obvious about it.*

"Is that so?" Elizabeth replied in a neutral voice.

"Oh yes. He is so charming and easygoing, and so well read! It's always a pleasure to visit Linden Park when he is here, for one is never bored.

"I would rather fancy him myself, except Mama says he's as poor as a church mouse and I really should set my sights higher." Annabel sighed. "Trouble is, all the richer men in the area have not near one whit his style. Even his brother, sweet as he is, is more focused on calves and crops than on clothes and dancing."

"Why are the younger Mr. Willoughby's pockets to let?" Elizabeth asked casually. "From this lovely home, it would appear that the Riverton family is not impoverished."

"I do not know." Annabel wrinkled her pretty, vacant brow. "Younger sons never seem to have much money, and as he is the youngest of four, I suppose they just ran out by the time they reached him!" She giggled at her weak joke.

"Yes, perhaps that is the case," Elizabeth murmured, but her attention was far from the conversation. It had been arrested by the sight of Spencer Willoughby spinning Mrs. Campbell as the dancers entered a particularly energetic part of the reel. The other woman's face was alight with laughter as Mr. Willoughby expertly turned her around. Elizabeth felt the unfamiliar stirrings of jealousy deep in her stomach. How she wished *she* were the one swirling about with Mr. Willoughby, his hands spanning her waist.

When she and Mr. Willoughby had danced, he had been all that was courteous and admirable. And yet, she had sensed a peculiar restraint in his touch, as though he had felt uncomfortable or restless in the traditional posture of the set.

It was most curious.

Perhaps he preferred the waltz, which had recently become the most fashionable dance in London. She had never danced it herself, although she had seen others do so.

How wonderful it would be to spend an entire dance in Mr. Willoughby's arms, their faces almost close enough to . . .

She forced herself to turn her attention to other things.

". . . marry an heiress as well," she heard Annabel saying.

"Pardon me?" she said. "My apologies, I'm afraid I was far away."

"I just said that young Mr. Willoughby is rather in the same situation as I am myself. He must marry a woman of wealth if he is to marry at all."

A woman of wealth. Someone such as herself, Elizabeth reflected. Yet again, a suspicion surfaced that his kindnesses toward her—and the spark of something more she had felt that night in the billiard room—could be nothing more than calculated attempts to capture a fat purse. Surely, a cultured, highborn man like Mr. Willoughby, even one with pockets to let, would have no other interest in a money-grubbing cit who could not even dance without tripping over her own feet.

Personal affairs did not differ, in the end, from business affairs, she thought. In business, she had to be constantly on her guard to ensure that no one took advantage of her. Others would take what they could, when they could, unless one was very careful.

She could not bring herself to believe that Mr. Willoughby was a bloodless fortune hunter. But had his warm touch and winning smiles simply turned her head?

Tired of debating this question with herself, Eliza-

beth brought her attention fully back to Miss Morrison
and switched the conversation to other, less depressing
matters.

Nine

Spencer still could not believe his good fortune. His meeting with Jonathan West, an elderly merchant with prodigious wealth and a fascination with science, had gone better than Spencer had dared dream. West had been excited about Spencer's experiments, and more than willing to bankroll him the funds he needed for six months' more work.

"Discoveries don't happen quickly, Mr. Willoughby, and I am willing to wait," Mr. West had said, handing Spencer a small stack of crisp banknotes. "I have precious little enough left in life to interest me, and anticipating your success will give me a reason to rise from my bed each morning. M'business runs itself, now, you know. Sons don't need their old father around, getting in the way. Glad to have the opportunity of a new challenge, where I can do some good."

Spencer had almost leaped across the desk and hugged the gruff old gentleman, and had had to restrain himself from running down Duke of York Street on his way to purchase new supplies. The euphoria of finally being free of debt—able to live once again within his means and free of the temptation to solicit funds from his brothers—had made him almost light-headed.

Once he had bought a substantial quantity of silver nitrate, along with tins of several other chemicals, he engaged a coach and transported the lot back to his rooms in St. James's. In his study, he searched through a stack of paper on a small escritoire to find the note he had scribbled in haste after meeting Patrick Shea at the Royal Exchange.

Finally, buried under bills and invitations, he found the scrap of paper. "Henry Cox, Cannon Street."

The mill owner's premises were easy to find, located as they were on a busy corner and marked with a large, freshly repainted sign.

After being ushered into the proprietor's office, Spencer found himself facing a pale, balding man who looked to be a decade older than himself. A fading but still angry-looking scar slashed across one temple. With a distracted smile, Mr. Cox rose from his desk and extended his left hand. The right one, Spencer noticed, was bound in bandages.

"Welcome, Mr. Willoughby. What may I do for you?"

"Thank you, Mr. Cox," Spencer replied, shaking the businessman's hand and then settling into the chair his host indicated. Cox resumed his seat behind the desk. "I hope you shall not think me impertinent, but I believe you and I have a common interest."

"Yes?" Mr. Cox's pale gray eyes were hooded.

"Are you acquainted with a gentleman named Victor Newfield?"

At this question, the other man bounded up from his chair, sending it backward with such force that it toppled over. "If you are another of Newfield's ruffians, you would be wise not to assault me on my own premises," he shouted. "My employees will not stand for it, and I will have you in jail!"

Spencer was dumbfounded by this outburst. What had Newfield done?

"I have no intention of doing you harm," he hastened

We'd Like to Invite You to Subscribe to Zebra's Regency Romance Book Club and Give You a Gift of 4 Free Books as Your Introduction! (Worth $19.96!)

If you're a Regency lover, imagine the joy of getting **4 FREE Zebra Regency Romances** and then the chance to have thes lovely stories delivered to your home each month at the lowest price available! Well, that's our offer to you and here': how you benefit by becoming a Regency Romance subscriber:

- **4 FREE Introductory Regency Romances are delivered to your doorstep (you only pay for shipping and handling)**

- **4 BRAND NEW Regencies are then delivered each month (usually before they're available in bookstores)**

- **Subscribers save almost $4.00 every month**

- **You also receive a FREE monthly newsletter, which features author profiles, discounts, subscriber benefits, book previews and more**

- **No risks or obligations...in other words, you can cancel whenever you wish with no questions asked**

Join the thousands of readers who enjoy the savings and convenience offered to Regency Romance subscribers. After your initial introductory shipment, you receive 4 brand-new Zebra Regency Romances each month to examine for 10 days. Then, if you decide to keep the books, you'll pay the preferred subscriber's price, plus shipping and handling.

It's a no-lose proposition, so return the FREE BOOK CERTIFICATE today!

Say Yes to 4 Free Books!
Complete and return the order card to receive this $19.96 value, ABSOLUTELY FREE!

If the certificate is missing below, write to:
Regency Romance Book Club
P.O. Box 5214, Clifton, New Jersey 07015-5214
or call TOLL-FREE 1-800-770-1963

Visit our website at www.kensingtonbooks.com.

FREE BOOK CERTIFICATE

YES! Please rush me 4 Zebra Regency Romances (I only pay for shipping and handling). I understand that each month thereafter I will be able to preview 4 brand-new Regency Romances FREE for 10 days. Then, if I should decide to keep them, I will pay the money-saving preferred subscriber's price for all 4...that's a savings of 20% off the publisher's price. I may return any shipment within 10 days and owe nothing, and I may cancel this subscription at any time. My 4 FREE books will be mine to keep in any case.

Name _____

Address _____ Apt. _____

City _____ State _____ Zip _____

Telephone ( ) _____

Signature _____
(If under 18, parent or guardian must sign.)

RN092A

Terms and prices subject to change. Orders subject to acceptance by Regency Romance Book Club.
Offer valid in U.S. only.

to assure the older man. "I have never even met Victor Newfield."

Cox relaxed slightly, but made no move to sit down.

"In fact, my only interest in him is seeing him brought to justice," Spencer continued. "He has been threatening a friend of mine, and I am trying to gather evidence against him."

The mill owner let out a sigh of relief. He turned and righted his chair with his good hand, then slumped into it.

"In that case, Mr. Willoughby, I would be most happy to help you. I have been trying to get Newfield arrested myself, but the demmed man appears to have vanished into the air. The scoundrel owes me almost eight thousand pounds."

"How did he come to acquire such a debt?"

"It is partly my own fault," Mr. Cox said in a wry voice. "Newfield tells a good tale, and he assured me that he was in the midst of a major expansion of his business. Said he was about to open a second shop in Bath. I sold him several lots of good winter wools, as well as some silks and a large quantity of other fabrics— on credit. I suspect he turned around and instantly resold them in the 'Change for a fraction of their value, in cash." Cox looked down at his desk, picked up a ruler, and turned it over idly.

Spencer, sensing the man's embarrassment at having been taken in, remained silent. After a few moments, Cox continued his story.

"Newfield regularly paid me a small portion of the total owed. He told me that it was taking time for the shop in Bath to attract a steady clientele, and that he would pay me the balance as soon as he could. I had seen his shop in the Strand, and it appeared most prosperous."

Cox sighed. "I was so anxious to acquire his custom that I misjudged him utterly."

"Do not berate yourself. Everyone makes mistakes."

Cox seemed not to have heard him. "Two weeks ago, I happened to be in Bath and made inquiries as to the location of Newfield's shop. No one there had ever heard of it."

Spencer nodded.

"I hastened back to London, and asked a clerk at his shop here for details of the Bath establishment. The clerk had no knowledge of such an operation, either."

Cox lapsed into another silence.

"What did you do next?" Spencer prompted him. "Did you confront Newfield with your suspicions?"

"I did not have the chance," Cox replied. "He was not in the shop when I called. But that night, I worked late, alone. As I locked up the office, two men in dark coats and mufflers approached me."

"And they were the cause of your injured face and hand?" Spencer guessed.

Cox nodded. "They warned me to make no further inquiries about any facet of Newfield's business, or to even think about buying an arrest warrant, or they would return."

At this revelation, Spencer felt both enraged and sick. Enraged that a man would stoop to such depths, and sick at the knowledge that Newfield's next target could be Miss Scott.

He hoped Ben and his father were keeping a very close watch on her, and he longed with every bone in his body to finish this meeting so that he could get back to Linden Park. But he needed Mr. Cox's information and cooperation, in case he ever came in direct confrontation with Newfield.

"So then you attempted to have him arrested?" Spencer asked.

"Well, it took a day or two before I was back on my feet and could see about obtaining an arrest warrant," Cox replied. "And by that time, Newfield had disappeared. When I went to ensure that he was there, one of the clerks in his shop informed me that he had left Town to handle some business affairs and had not specified a date when he would return."

"I believe I know what those affairs were," Spencer replied. After swearing the other man to secrecy, he revealed only as much of Elizabeth's story as necessary to illuminate the situation for Mr. Cox, leaving out her name and any identifying details.

When he finished his story, Cox exploded. "Newfield is an utter fiend! Not only to have me attacked, but to roughly use a young woman as well." His voice shook.

"We think alike on that count," Spencer replied grimly.

"So how can I assist you?" Cox asked.

"In several ways," Spencer said. He suppressed an urge to get up from his chair and walk about Cox's small office, the better to collect his thoughts. "First, you should make the Bow Street Runners aware of your encounter with Newfield's men."

"Already done. The Runners have noted the condition of my face and hand. There was also a witness, a man who works in the building next door, and he spoke with Bow Street as well."

"Good." Spencer drummed his fingers on the arm of his chair. "Next, I think you should send word—not in a letter, but verbally, through a messenger—to Newfield's premises. He must have a manager in charge while he is absent."

Cox nodded.

"Have the messenger inform the manager that you plan to absolve Newfield of all his debts to you."

At this suggestion, his companion's jaw fell. "Absolve

him? After the way his men mistreated me?" he spluttered.

"I do not mean that you should actually forgive his debts," Spencer explained. "Just give him reason to think that you will."

"But a man's word is his bond," Cox responded. "I cannot lie about such a matter."

"You will not have to. Your messenger shall say the words."

"But what is the point of doing such a thing?"

Spencer felt admiration for the mill owner, who was clearly disturbed by the thought of dealing dishonestly with anyone, even a man who had so clearly abused him.

"It is a trick to lure Newfield back to London, and to ensure that he stays here long enough that you can have him arrested. If he believes his largest creditor has succumbed to his pressure and absolved him of his debt, he will have no reason to avoid his offices."

Cox hesitated, then seemed to accept the logic of this plan.

"You are right, of course," the older man conceded. "If I am ever to have any hope of seeing that money, I must be able to catch Newfield."

"Thank you. I appreciate your help in this matter. Please send word to me at Linden Park if you learn anything of Newfield's current whereabouts."

"Believe me, Mr. Willoughby, I will. If we are lucky, his next known address will be a sheriff's sponging house!"

Both men permitted themselves a dry laugh.

Spencer scooped a measure of silver salts onto his scales and smiled. His carefully guarded tin of supplies had been replenished to the brim, and he had two larger containers of the precious substance stored under his workbench. Finally, he had the materials he needed to conduct a full series of experiments. He was determined to repay Mr. West's faith in him. He *would* make this photographic process work.

As he recorded in his notebook the quantities of chemicals he was using today, he remembered his promise to explain his work to Miss Scott when he returned from London. He had arrived home too late last evening to see her, although he had quickly reassured himself, in a late-night conversation with his father, that she was safe and that Victor had not appeared.

He would be most relieved when Mr. Mason had finished his work and Miss Scott was legally protected from Newfield's grasp, he thought, as he closed the notebook and returned it to the shelf. It irked him to wait at Linden Park like a helpless hare, fearing that a baying hound would soon arrive to pounce.

But there was no other sensible course of action. Here, Miss Scott could be well protected by the family and the household staff. And here, she could meet conveniently with Mr. Mason. If she began moving about the countryside, it would take longer for her affairs to be settled.

No, much as it annoyed him to wait and not to act, remaining quietly at Linden Park was the only logical solution.

Earlier this morning, Miss Scott had not yet risen by the time Spencer had eaten a quick breakfast and hurried out to his workroom. He had barely been able to contain his eagerness to return to his work, partly because he was keen to experiment with his new materials, and partly because the work provided a convenient distraction from his concerns about Victor Newfield.

He would, however, make a point of returning to the house for nuncheon. It would be very good to see Miss Scott again.

He transferred the chemicals to a small beaker and

leaned below the work top to scoop a ladle of rainwater from a small pail on the floor. As he worked, he found his mind drifting back to Miss Scott. He remembered the warmth of her smile as he had led her through the steps of the country dance, her eagerness to partner him although it was clear she felt uncomfortable on the dance floor. She was easily the most arresting woman there that night, he thought, comparing her to the sweet but simpering Miss Morrison and the garrulous Mrs. Campbell.

Perhaps, just perhaps, if this experiment worked, he would be able to show Miss Scott that he was much more than a highborn fribble.

Fired with new resolve, he turned back to his worktable.

But three hours later, as the sun rose higher in the sky and his stomach had begun to growl in anticipation of nuncheon, he slapped his hand against the rough wooden table in frustration. The latest combination of chemicals had been no more efficacious than his other solutions. The leather square he had exposed the week before and stored carefully in the lead-lined box had turned just as black as all the rest.

Perhaps he was just a dilettante after all.

He was if he gave up so easily. Even Mr. West understood that these things took time. Spencer had read enough scientific history to know that to be true.

But he didn't have much time to prove himself to Miss Scott, he thought, as he carefully poured his latest solution of used muriatic acid into a second pail reserved for that purpose. If Mr. Mason properly did his work, she would likely disappear back to London within a week or two. Their worlds, which had converged for such a brief period of time, would separate again.

Shaking his head at the foolish turn of his thoughts, Spencer bent over his notebook to record the results of his latest experiment. So absorbed was he in this work that he didn't hear two people approaching until a high, feminine laugh reached his ears.

He turned to see Maisie, the Linden Park servant serving as Miss Scott's maid, chatting with a young stable hand named Frank. From the delight on her face, it was evident that the two were more than just passing acquaintances in the Riverton household. The pair soon moved out of his line of sight, probably off to a shadowy corner of the barn. Spencer grinned.

His grin widened when Elizabeth slipped into his workroom.

"So this is where you hide during the day!" she exclaimed, settling onto the milking stool.

"Yes, you have uncovered my lair." In an absence of just a few days, he had partly forgotten how tempting she was. This morning, as usual, a few stray chestnut curls had escaped from her chignon and fallen about her shoulders. She was wearing a perfectly respectable rose-colored day dress that nonetheless clung most charmingly to her. For such a petite woman, she was remarkably curvaceous, he thought, not for the first time. A tingle such as he had not felt in years suffused his lower limbs, and other places.

"Have you come to find out more about my experiments?" he asked in a loud, strangled voice. It was as though he were trying to prevent her from reading his thoughts. He prayed she did not remark on his odd manner.

"Yes, I am most curious." Seemingly ignorant of his discomfort, she leaned forward from her perch to look at the chemicals arrayed on his work top. "What sorts of materials do you use?"

For the next few minutes, he explained the nature of his work. Much to his gratification, she displayed none of Benjamin's skepticism. Indeed, her questions were most intelligent and displayed a good general knowledge of his field.

"And how are your efforts progressing?"

"I had been stalled for lack of funds," he admitted reluctantly. "I was using almost all of my income to finance my experiments. But due to a recent bit of luck, I suspect that all my monetary troubles are a thing of the past."

He told her about his meeting with Jonathan West, and the new materials he had purchased in London. "So now the research should progress swimmingly," he concluded.

"I am pleased that you have the money you need for your work," she said with warmth. And, indeed, she looked overjoyed, a wide grin creasing her face.

It was most pleasant to share his enthusiasm with someone who showed such support for his work.

They discussed his project for several more minutes, and then Spencer felt compelled to ask the question that had been dogging him since she first came to the workroom. "How did you come to know so much about optics?"

Elizabeth lowered her eyes in an uncharacteristically shy gesture, and he noted a faint blush staining her cheeks. "While you were in London, your parents were kind enough to allow me access to the Linden Park library. There, I discovered several books and monographs on the subject. I did not want to come to you as a green girl full of ill-informed questions."

"Truly, Miss Scott, you are a woman outside my experience," he said, not caring that his admiration was clearly evident in his voice. "I cannot think of another female who would have gone to the trouble."

"I suppose it is in my nature," she replied, swinging one slippered foot below her. Inadvertently, he was sure, she thus gave him a glimpse of an exceedingly well-turned ankle. "In my work, I always research my partners and competitors fully. It does not do to enter a discussion unprepared."

"And do you consider me a partner or a competitor?" he asked, keeping his voice light.

"I consider you neither," she said. As she raised her eyes to his, he saw the flush intensify on her normally pale skin. "I consider you a friend."

"As I do you," he replied, aware of a sudden tension in the cluttered room. He hesitated even to breathe, as though that might break the invisible bridge that had sprung up between them.

They remained silent for a moment. Involuntarily, he moved closer to her. The rosewater scent he associated with her enveloped him, displacing the harsh smells of chemicals and horses.

She looked up at him, several emotions he could not identify seemingly warring on her face. A frown swept by, to be replaced by a tentative smile, which in turn disappeared as she began to nibble on her bottom lip in a most innocently provocative manner. She said nothing, but continued to gaze at him with those sensational green eyes.

God help him, but he was lost.

"I did not expect to see you out in the barn consorting with the servants, Elizabeth, but I suppose I should not be surprised. After all, you always did have common tastes," a male voice drawled from beyond the door. A few seconds later, Victor Newfield strolled casually into the tiny workroom. Spencer watched, aghast, as the appealing blush vanished from Elizabeth's cheeks and her face turned a deathly gray.

Ten

She should have known he would have the luck to find her quickly. If he could run her to ground in little-known Chapel Street, it only stood to reason that he could track her to Linden Park.

"I am no servant, and I will thank you not to malign Miss Scott's character under my family's roof." Spencer's voice was icy as he turned to face the intruder.

"I have come not to malign Miss Scott, but to take her away," Victor replied with the unpleasant laugh that had haunted Elizabeth's nightmares.

"Come now, my dear." He addressed her in a sickly sweet voice she had never heard before. "It is only natural to experience some nervousness before a wedding. Come back to London with me now, and we can talk about it."

Elizabeth began to review her options one by one, just as she would during business meetings. Victor obviously planned to remove her, and she didn't doubt he would use force if necessary. Was there anything she could use as a weapon?

Casting her eyes about the workroom, she spied an old whip still hanging from a nail in the wall, from the days when this area was still part of the tack room. Good.

But what if she could not overpower him? Mr. Willoughby would come to her aid, of that she was certain. But Victor was a more than able foe, even for two people.

Whatever his many faults, his one advantage was that he was in superb physical shape.

If they could not prevent him from capturing her again, she would need to think of a way to escape his carriage.

". . . after all, we do love each other, don't we, darling?"

Victor's oily voice finally penetrated her thoughts. The thought that he would even claim that she loved him shook her out of her preoccupation with strategies. Her heart pounding as fear, indignation, and anger engulfed her, she spoke for the first time since he had entered the room.

"I have seen rats in the London sewers that I loved more than I would ever love you, you loathsome cretin." She fixed him with her best subdue-the-employees stare.

"Now, now, darling, stop having fun at my expense."

"No, Victor, you stop putting on this ridiculous show. Mr. Willoughby knows the story."

"The entire story?" Victor drawled, leaning against the door frame.

Elizabeth barely restrained herself from gasping. Victor would not reveal the secret of her parentage to Mr. Willoughby, would he? The thought that Mr. Willoughby would know of her illegitimate birth, and think less of her as a result, hurt almost as much as the idea that Victor would succeed in forcing her to the altar.

Victor's knowledge of her heritage was the only hold he had over her, she reassured herself. He would be a fool to play his trump card now.

And yet, Victor was not exactly the brightest man in England, she thought. Elizabeth had to convince him that Spencer already knew the whole truth.

"Yes, the *entire* story," she retorted, stealing a glance at Mr. Willoughby. However, he was not looking at her. He was staring at Victor in an assessing manner.

"Well, that saves me a lot of bother, does it not?" Victor's voice returned to its usual caustic timbre. "I can just toss you into my carriage like the baggage you are."

"That is enough." Spencer spoke up from his corner. "I believe, Mr. Newfield, that you have had a chance to say what you came to say. Miss Scott obviously does not wish to return to London with you, so I must ask you to leave."

"You can ask all you like, but somehow I doubt you will be able to stop me." Victor eyed the slighter man up and down, his insolence obvious.

Elizabeth's fury grew. "Victor, please . . ."

Mr. Willoughby wasted no further time with words. In an action so fast Elizabeth almost did not see it, he struck the larger man, knocking Victor's head sideways.

Her cousin stumbled, almost losing his footing. He regained his feet, however, and glared at Mr. Willoughby, his eyes alight with a dangerous gleam Elizabeth knew all too well.

"You are an idiot to challenge me," he roared. "But if you truly enjoy being pulped, I will be happy to oblige."

"Victor, no!" Elizabeth cried. "Stop!"

"It is fine, Miss Scott. I am not afraid to fight." Spencer tried to imbue his voice with a confidence he did not feel.

Newfield towered over him by a good six inches and must have outweighed him by at least three stone. And it was fights such as the one he had begun that had resulted in many days spent in the infirmary at Harrow.

But he would be damned if he would back down in front of Miss Scott.

All bullies were cowards at heart. They only bullied people they thought they could best.

Victor struck back with a clean upper cut. *He certainly seems to think he can best me,* Spencer thought as he staggered back against the workbench. The metallic taste of blood filled his mouth.

Rage against Newfield surged through him. He would make this scoundrel pay for terrifying Elizabeth, even if he died in the attempt.

Growling, he pushed off the workbench and swung at his opponent. Newfield moved at the last minute, and the blow glanced off his arm.

Damn. Spencer darted sideways to regroup.

"Run all you like, runt. You cannot get away from me." Victor lunged, but Spencer ducked and the larger man stumbled. He might be massive, but Spencer had the advantage of agility.

Before Newfield had fully found his feet, Spencer clipped him soundly on the jaw.

Victor howled and swung back wildly, connecting with Spencer's cheek. Spencer felt his head snap back, and his brain began to buzz.

He shook his head, trying to clear it. As if from a great distance, he heard Miss Scott crying for them to stop.

"I will go with him," she cried. "I will do anything. Just stop this foolishness!"

"You shall not go with him while I am still standing." Spencer momentarily shifted his focus from Victor to Elizabeth. And what he saw horrified him.

Miss Scott was standing on the milking stool, which she had obviously just used to reach an old whip from the wall above her head. She now held the battered ivory handle with its long leather lash.

"Miss Scott, please leave!" he shouted, hoping she would turn to go before Newfield realized what she had in mind.

It was a forlorn hope. Victor, following Spencer's line of sight, turned and saw his cousin poised to strike him with the whip.

"You thankless baggage!" With one swift move, Victor clenched her slim wrist, forcing her to release her hold on the whip. It clattered to the dusty floor, and he stooped to pick it up.

"If you are so fond of whips, perhaps you would like a taste of leather yourself," he growled.

Victor's words lit a fire of fury in Spencer that he had not known himself capable of. Hurling himself across the room, he began raining blows on the other man's upper body: cheeks, chin, shoulder, chest. Victor returned the favor in kind.

They tumbled to the floor, and Victor pinned him, facedown, with one massive knee lodged in the small of his back. Spencer inhaled a mouthful of sawdust and spluttered.

"Since you seem resistant to the idea of my touching dear Miss Scott with this whip, perhaps you would prefer I try it out on you?" Victor gave the whip an experimental crack just inches from the tip of Spencer's nose.

Spencer thrashed sideways, but the much heavier man had immobilized him completely.

How humiliating, to be literally horsewhipped in front of Miss Scott. Spencer reached backward to punch Newfield in the kneecap. The blow glanced off his opponent's leg, doing no harm.

"The whip seems to work very well on the floor," Victor said in a mocking voice. "Let's see how well it works on a real old nag."

Blinding pain ripped through Spencer as the whip seared his shoulders once, then again. Dimly, he heard Elizabeth bolt from the room, shouting for help. He did not care any longer whether anyone came to witness his indignity. He only cared about besting this scoundrel until he cried for mercy.

And since Victor had decided to fight unfairly, Spencer had no compunction about doing the same. With a quick twist, he grabbed the foot Victor was using to brace himself on the workroom floor, and yanked with all his might.

To his immense pleasure, Victor crashed to the floor with a yelp of pain.

Quickly pressing his advantage, Spencer sprang to his feet. He barely felt the flaming ache in his shoulders, so white hot was his rage.

Sprinting to the other side of the room, he grabbed the bucket of used muriatic acid from beneath the workbench. As the heavier man struggled to his feet, Spencer flung the contents of the pail toward his tormentor's legs. As the corrosive chemicals hit him, Victor bellowed in agony and toppled back to the floor.

"Damn you, what sort of water is that?" he screamed as he brought his ungloved hands to his shins, attempting to brush the acid from his trousers. He bellowed anew as the substance stung his palms.

"Just a little cocktail I mixed up especially for you," Spencer said. "Let it never be said I am not a hospitable host."

"You dirty coward!" Victor spat. "I thought that *gentlemen* were supposed to fight fair."

"And do you call whipping a prone man fair?" Elizabeth cried as she rushed back into the room, followed by Benjamin and Lord Riverton. "I knew you were wretched, Victor, but I had no idea you would stoop to such depths."

Benjamin quickly took in the scene, with Newfield writhing on the floor and Spencer, now gasping for air, leaning against the worktop. He let out a low whistle.

"Don't know how you managed it, Spence, but you seem to have bested this giant." The admiration in his voice would have been gratifying, Spencer reflected, if it had not been laced with doubt.

"I suppose my dancing skills stood me in good stead.

After all, this required a little fancy footwork." Spencer picked a rag off the counter and used it to stanch the blood flowing from a corner of his lip.

"Good heavens, Mr. Willoughby, you are bleeding." Elizabeth rushed across the room. Picking up a somewhat cleaner rag from the table, she gently pried away the sodden one and began dabbing at the wound. Despite his pain, Spencer felt an ache of pleasure at her gentle touch.

"I am so sorry that you have been injured on my behalf. This is absolutely dreadful. I should never have come here. It was foolish, stupid, bullheaded . . ."

"You were right to come here," he said, interrupting the flow of words, grasping her small hand. "It was my pleasure to help."

He glanced around her at Victor, who was slowly rising from the floor. "It really was a pleasure, knocking you down," he said to his opponent in a conversational tone. "But if you ever come within a mile of Linden Park again, I shall have you arrested."

"On what charge?" Victor howled.

"Attempted kidnapping, for one."

To his surprise, Victor laughed. It was a dry, mirthless sound. "And how, may I ask, am I to be charged with kidnapping Miss Scott? She is my betrothed, and I have the legal right to take her where I will."

Elizabeth gasped.

Spencer shot his gaze back to Miss Scott. What was going on here? It was incomprehensible that Miss Scott had affianced herself to this madman.

"Is this true? Are you legally betrothed to Mr. Newfield?" How on earth had a crude man like Newfield ever drawn any sort of interest from a refined gentlewoman like Miss Scott?

"He wishes it were so!" she cried.

So it was a lie? Spencer felt a wave of cool relief

wash over him—a relief that vanished with Newfield's next words.

"I wish it were so?" Victor exploded. "You accepted my offer. I heard you!"

"Mr. Newfield coerced me into this so-called betrothal." Miss Scott turned to Spencer, and her words tumbled out in a rush.

"He threatened to blackmail me, to shame my aunts, to ruin my business. There are no witnesses to my verbal acceptance, and there is no written proof. There have been no banns read, as I asked the vicar of my parish not to accept any such request. Victor has no evidence with which to sue me for breach of promise, especially—" She stopped, evidently remembering not to reveal to Victor that she was in the midst of legal action to protect her inheritance.

"What were you going to say?" Victor croaked.

Miss Scott hesitated for no more than a fraction of a second. She must be a demmed skilled business negotiator, Spencer thought.

"Especially since it would be clear to any judge who met me that I would never marry you, you vile creature."

"Then why did you agree to marry me in the first place, if I am so vile?" Victor's face was puce, and a vein throbbed on his thick neck.

"To stop you from hauling me off to Gretna Green like a trapped animal." Miss Scott's chin was raised in defiance, but Spencer thought he detected a glimmer of fear in her large green eyes. "At least it gave me a few weeks' grace, in the guise of planning the ceremony."

Victor struggled to his feet, and immediately bent forward to massage his shins. They must be burning in agony, Spencer thought with satisfaction.

"I brought an end to that plan," Victor muttered, glaring at Elizabeth. "If you had only stayed in my carriage last week, instead of leaping out into traffic like some imbecile from Bedlam, I would have had you before a cleric with no fuss whatsoever."

"If you think you shall convince me to marry you now, you are greatly mistaken, Victor. I had no desire to do so in the first place. Your abduction of me in Chapel Street was reprehensible. And your attack on Mr. Willoughby has done nothing to improve my opinion of your character. I suggest you leave. Nothing you can say or do will convince me to go with you."

"I did not plan to convince you," Newfield muttered. "I planned to *take* you."

Miss Scott said nothing. Her stance remained defiant, although her hands began, almost imperceptibly, to shake.

Spencer felt an unholy urge to pour the remainder of his muriatic acid on Newfield's head.

"If I were you, Newfield, I would get myself to a doctor quickly for some salve," he said with deceptive mildness. "Those chemicals can do great damage to one's skin if they're left on too long."

Miss Scott's cousin stared at Spencer, hatred filming his dull eyes. He dusted off his frayed black overcoat and strode toward the door.

"And I meant what I said, Newfield. Come within a mile of Linden Park, and I shall have the magistrate here so quickly it will make your head spin—if not for kidnapping, then for assault."

"Runts like you always go crying to the law," Victor said with a sneer. "Bloody toffs. You can bluster all you like, but she is legally mine." With that, he pushed past Ben and Lord Riverton, and hobbled out of the barn.

With Victor disposed of for the time being, Spencer turned his attention back to Miss Scott. She was sitting on the milking stool, gaze cast downward, twisting the bloodstained rag in her hands.

There were so many things he wanted to say—to whisper, to yell, to ask—that he could not decide which to voice first. Was she all right? What did she want to do now? And why, for the love of God, had she not told him about the betrothal?

She continued to stare at the floor. Far away, at the other end of the barn, he heard a horse whicker.

One of the bystanders coughed.

Finally, she raised her head.

"Miss Scott, I don't believe I know the *entire* story," Spencer drawled.

Eleven

"There, Mr. Willoughby, I think that should do it."
Aunt Louisa smoothed the last of her pungent, home-
made ointment over the raw skin of his shoulders. "Does
it feel any better?"

"Yes, very much so. Thank you, Mrs. Timms. You
have worked miracles. I told my mother there was no
need to call a physician, and I believe I was right." Mr.
Willoughby winced as he straightened up on the low
wooden kitchen chair, and Elizabeth felt her heart contract.

This was all her fault. If she had never taken the whip
from the wall—never mind that, if she had never come
to Linden Park—Mr. Willoughby would be happily
working on his invention instead of sitting in this over-
heated kitchen wracked with pain.

Her aunt had strenuously objected to Elizabeth's presence in the kitchen. The older woman had dismissed all
the servants so that she could work in peace, and she
had declared that her niece's presence was both unnec-
essary and unseemly. But Elizabeth had been adamant:
Mr. Willoughby's injuries were entirely her fault, and she
would do whatever she could to help him now.

In the end, it turned out she could do little but heat
up ingredients and stir the mixtures in various pots ac-
cording to Aunt Louisa's instructions. This she did with
enthusiasm, but it was precious little.

She had offered to apply the salve to Mr. Willoughby's shoulders, but both her aunt and her protector had turned such shocked eyes toward her at that suggestion that she had hastily retracted it, her face aflame with embarrassment at her boldness.

It was terribly bothersome being an unmarried woman, she reflected. It so restricted one's activities.

Now, however, as Aunt Louisa gathered up her tools and ingredients, Elizabeth stole one last, surreptitious look at Mr. Willoughby.

It was despicable to be thinking such things at such a time, but she could not help but notice that Spencer Willoughby was a most attractive man. It was rare that she had ever seen a man in such a state of dishabille. Indeed, the only similar occasion she could recall was a day at the company warehouse when she had come upon an employee who had fallen off a dock. He had been drying his clothes, and himself, in a disused office. That episode had ended with much blushing, stammering, and slamming of doors.

But even without a broad range of knowledge of the male form, Elizabeth was willing to guess that Spencer Willoughby was particularly attractive. His forearms and chest were lightly dusted with pale gold hairs, and his shoulders were surprisingly muscular for one so slim. His back tapered most appealingly toward his snug pantaloons. Even though she had been able to do little to help him, she was not sorry she had come to the kitchen.

Aunt Louisa put a pair of scissors back into the small cloth bag she always carried when she traveled. "Are you able to get dressed again?" she asked her patient.

Mr. Willoughby nodded.

"Come along, then, Elizabeth, and give Mr. Willoughby some privacy," Aunt Louisa commanded over her shoulder, as she made her ponderous way through the doorway.

"Yes, Aunt Louisa," Elizabeth responded, as she followed her elderly relative.

At the door, however, she heard a low moan. Turning back, she saw Mr. Willoughby grimacing as he reached for an old linen shirt warming on a stool by the hearth.

"I do not believe you are fine at all," Elizabeth murmured as she moved back into the room. It was highly improper to be here alone with Mr. Willoughby, but it seemed most callous to leave him in pain when she could help. She tamped down the rogue thought that it was also most pleasant to be here alone with him—despite the fact that he was, in all likelihood, furious with her.

"May I help you put on your shirt?"

"Yes, Miss Scott, thank you. I suspect I may have overestimated my capabilities." He sank back onto the chair.

She retrieved the shirt from the hearth, and shook it to cool it a bit so that it would not irritate Mr. Willoughby's injured shoulders. "I really think you should have seen a doctor about your wounds," she said as she bunched up the right sleeve of the shirt and drew it over his bruised hand.

"Truly, Miss Scott, I am fine. In pain, yes, but I do not think anything is broken. And your aunt's salve is already starting to work." He grimaced as he raised his arm so that she could pull the sleeve up it.

"All the same, it would be terrible if these cuts became infected." As she drew the shirt over his shoulder, the side of her hand brushed his skin. Mr. Willoughby shivered.

"Oh, Mr. Willoughby, I apologize!" she cried, assuming she had touched one of his welts. "I did not mean to cause you pain. More pain, that is."

"You did not hurt me, truly," he said in an oddly strangled voice. "It is no matter."

An awkward silence hung between them as she eased

the shirt across his shoulders and thrust his left arm into the other sleeve. She circled in front of him to begin doing up the tortoiseshell buttons, willing her mind not to think about the inappropriateness of this situation. Mr. Willoughby must have been thinking of it, however, for he stayed her hand.

"Thank you, Miss Scott, but I can handle this part of the task myself." Slowly, he began fastening the shirt-front.

Elizabeth turned once more to go, then stopped and pivoted as she reached the door. "I am so sorry, Mr. Willoughby," she whispered. "This is all my fault. I was an idiot to come here, to put you and your family in the midst of my troubles."

"Please do not trouble yourself on that account, Miss Scott. As I said in the barn, I could not leave you in such desperate straits. There is no fault for which to be sorry." Carefully, he began to tuck his shirttails into the waistband of his black pantaloons.

"Well, there is still at least one. I cannot believe I was so foolish as to take that whip from the barn wall. Victor is so dense, he likely would never have even noticed it if I had not practically handed it to him." A vision of Victor looming over Mr. Willoughby, brandishing the whip, appeared in her mind's eye. She suspected it would be many years, if ever, before she could rid herself of that horrifying image.

Mr. Willoughby frowned. "Why did you reach for the whip, Miss Scott? Although Newfield is much larger than I, I was more than willing and able to take him on. Did you think me so incompetent that you had to help?" The emotional pain writ on his face at that moment looked even more intense than the physical pain that she was sure was throbbing across his shoulders.

"No, of course not, Mr. Willoughby!" she cried, stung that he would think she had so little faith in him. But

then, she realized, everyone else around him seemed reluctant to believe in his abilities. She remembered Lady
Riverton's dismissive words about his inventions, and
Benjamin's amazement in the barn that his brother had
bested Victor.

The thought that she might be just another naysayer
tore at her, and she struggled to explain what had made
her try to intervene.

"I am used to taking charge of situations—particularly
those that are of my own making," she began.

"Miss Scott, you must not blame—"

Cutting him off, she continued doggedly. "In our
household, my aunts defer to me. At work, all the employees, even the senior ones, seek my opinion and guid-
ance. I have made decisions that have created work for
dozens of men, caused ships to set sail, and made for-
tunes for investors. I know it is unnatural, but it is simply
not in my nature to stand by weeping while a crisis un-
folds."

He nodded, but she was not sure if he accepted her
explanation or not. It was the truth. She desperately
hoped he believed it.

As another silence grew between them, she came to
a decision.

"I should leave today, now, and let Victor know by
letter that I have removed myself to another location,"
she announced, her heart hammering at the very thought
of any further contact with her cousin, no matter how
distant. Her stomach roiled, but she forced herself to continue. "No one else shall be hurt because of my stub-
bornness and stupidity."

"You cannot possibly leave yourself open to the risk
that he will find you!" Mr. Willoughby winced as he
rose from his chair and began to slowly cross the room
toward her. "The man is an animal. There is no telling
what he might do to you if you were wed."

"That is no matter. This disaster is of my own making, and I should be the one to take the consequences. Not you, nor anyone else." Her stomach churned at the thought of becoming Victor's bride, but she could not abide the thought of placing anyone else in danger on her behalf.

"Is it your fault that Victor is trying to blackmail you?" Mr. Willoughby's voice was soft as he reached the spot where she stood.

"No, of course not. But it is my fault that I left my affairs so haphazard for so long. And it is my fault that I gave in to his threats and agreed to a betrothal. I regret concealing that from you, too." Despair swept through her. Mr. Willoughby had every right to be furious with her for her deception.

"I must admit, I was most startled to hear that Newfield believed you were betrothed. Why did you not tell me?" Mr. Willoughby's face was unreadable.

"I would have told you, but I thought it might make you reluctant to help me," Elizabeth mumbled.

"What sort of man did you think I was, that I would leave you in distress?" His blue eyes narrowed.

"I did not know you when we met at the earl's wedding," she burst out. "I was desperate to accept your offer of help, as I had run out of options. And most men would be loath to interfere in another man's betrothal, no matter how irregular."

"I am not most men," he murmured, moving a step closer to her.

"That I have come to learn," she replied, transfixed by the indefinable expression in his eyes.

"In fact, I do find myself most willing to interfere in another man's betrothal," he said, continuing to regard her.

His focus on her began to make Elizabeth self-conscious. She had never in her life been assessed with such intensity, not even by the most formidable of business foes. And never in a business meeting had she been suffused with the warmth that seemed to seep from her chest to every extremity under Mr. Willoughby's gaze.

"You do?" she whispered inanely.

He did not answer her. Instead, he gently raised one bandaged hand to her face.

She stared at him, unable to breathe.

Carefully, as though afraid of frightening her, he touched her hair, then moved his hand to her shoulder. She could swear she felt his palm scald her through the light day dress she wore.

She inhaled a shaky breath and stayed utterly still.

What on earth am I doing? Spencer thought wildly as he caressed Elizabeth Scott. This was madness. If they were caught, she would be compromised. And he was no match for a woman such as she.

"I know this is most improper, Miss Scott. I do apologize," he murmured. But he could not pull his hand away.

"There is no need to apologize, Mr. Willoughby," she said with a small smile. "If I wished you to stop, I would say so."

He laughed out loud in astonishment. "You are, without a doubt, the most forthright woman I have ever met."

"It is a skill that has served me well in business. It has been invaluable in helping me get what I want."

"And what do you want now?"

She paused. And then, to his further astonishment, she placed her slim white arms very cautiously around his neck and leaned her cool forehead against him. She was so close that the rosewater scent she always wore enveloped them both.

He needed no further invitation. There was no hope for them, no future. He could offer her nothing, and they lived in two different worlds. But all of that did not seem to matter at the moment.

With a groan that was only slightly due to the pain wracking his back, he gathered her slight form into his arms. Her chignon, always a haphazard affair at best, began to come loose from its pins, tumbling down around her pale shoulders. Ecstatically, he ran his hands through her chestnut curls.

"You are so beautiful," he said in a ragged voice. Then he gave up the fight and lowered his lips to hers. He heard her sharp intake of breath and exulted that she was as eager for him as he was for her.

She tasted as sweet as he had suspected she would. And she was no timid maid, either. What she lacked in experience, she made up for in enthusiasm, kissing him back ardently.

As they parted to breathe, she reached up to trace her finger along the side of his stubbled face. Then, with infinite tenderness, she stretched toward him and kissed him.

Desire consumed Spencer as he returned her kiss. He had never wanted a woman so much in his life. After what seemed like many minutes, he ended the kiss so they could once again draw breath.

Blindly, he skimmed his hands over her slim shoulders and down the lace that framed her throat. Moving lower, he marveled yet again that such a slim woman could be so temptingly curvaceous.

He stroked his thumb across the thin muslin of her dress. As she gave a small moan of pleasure and arched toward him, he thought he would go mad. Perhaps he already was mad.

"Oh, Mr. Willoughby," she whispered.

He leaned back from her, looked her in the eye, and grinned.

"Under the circumstances, Miss Scott, may I invite you to call me Spencer?"

She laughed, a musical sound that both delighted him and broke the unusual mood that had wrapped around them both in the deserted kitchen. "Only if you agree to call me Elizabeth. Or Mary, as the case may be." Her face was flushed, her eyes alight.

He took in her disheveled hair, her radiant smile, her cheeks slightly reddened by the stubble on his own. What on earth had he done?

As he came back to his senses, Spencer cursed himself. He was truly a wretch, having fun with an innocent such as Miss Scott. She was a sheltered young woman, not some London actress accustomed to the ways of the world. What must she think? What must she expect now?

Marriage, he suspected. Honor demanded that he should offer for her now.

But marrying him would be almost as foolish a move on her part as marrying Victor. All he possessed were some tins of chemicals and his meager rented rooms in St. James's. She could do much, much better than a skinny, impoverished fourth son.

"Elizabeth it is, then," he said with a lightness that, for once, he did not feel. "I do apologize again. It was most barbaric of me to take advantage of you in this way."

"You did not take advantage of me, Spencer," she replied. She smiled as she said his name. "If anything, I took advantage of you. After all, you are an injured man."

He gave a bark of laughter.

"And since no one saw us, there is no harm done. We can go on as before."

She was going to give him an escape route. She was not going to force him to offer for her. And, by God, although he hated himself, he was going to grasp the lifeline she offered. To do else could chain her for life to a feckless, penniless inventor. He could not do that to her.

"Yes, you are most reasonable, Elizabeth. We shall go on just as before," he said, trying to imbue his voice with certainty.

Elizabeth's toes curled inside her kid slippers as the scene in the kitchen came to life again in her mind's eye.

It had been wrong, what they had done. Improper and inappropriate. But she found she could not regret one moment of her encounter with Spencer in the dim firelight.

Closing her eyes, she could feel once more his arms clasping her to him, his chest warm and solid against her. She could smell sandalwood, mixed with the sharp odor of salve. She could feel his lips sliding against hers. . . .

This would not do. She must focus on the matter at hand. Resolutely, she opened her eyes and forced herself back to the present moment. She glanced around at the assembled company, still feeling somewhat dazed. The first thing that caught her attention was Mr. Willoughby's voice.

"We all want to keep you safe, Miss Scott, but this sham betrothal makes things more complicated." Spencer was in what Elizabeth had come to realize was his thinking mode. He paced back and forth in front of the large marble fireplace in the drawing room.

"I do apologize again for keeping that part of the story a secret." Elizabeth sighed, and silently berated herself for her foolishness. "I think I was trying to deny it to myself. But I never intended to follow through on it."

Now that she had begun this confession, she raced to get the words out. "I know that sounds abominable, but

I really did not know what else to do. He coerced me into agreeing to a betrothal just two weeks ago, only a few days before he abducted me in Chapel Street." She shuddered at the memory.

Spencer looked up sharply when she said "two weeks ago," but when he did not say anything, she continued her story.

"I had been too clever by half. I thought that, with the few months' grace the false betrothal would afford me, I could get my affairs in order. I told Victor I wanted to keep our agreement a secret as long as possible—that an early announcement would decrease the value of the company. It was nonsense, but he is so greedy that he believed it, at least for a few days. That is why there was no notice in the newspapers, and no banns read. I truly believed that I would be able to cry off, with no harm done."

She glanced around the room to see what effect this shocking announcement would have on the entire complement of the two families who had gathered to find a solution to this latest dilemma. To her immense relief, she saw only sympathy and understanding writ there, although Aunt Louisa's round face was creased with worry.

"So you never wanted to marry him?" Spencer's voice was intense, and his gaze bored into hers as though they were the only two people in the room.

"Never!" Elizabeth flinched at the sound of her own raised voice.

"We have loathed each other since we were children," she continued in a quieter tone. "I only agreed to his ridiculous offer in an attempt to keep Aunt Harriet and Aunt Louisa safe from scandal. Victor has been . . . blackmailing me with a family secret. On my own behalf, I do not care. But I will not allow the scandal to touch my family or to harm my business."

Please, please don't let anyone ask the nature of the scandal. And please don't let Aunt Louisa blurt it out.

"What devilish fustian!" Aunt Harriet exclaimed, jumping into the breach with one of Roger Scott's favorite expressions. Elizabeth could have kissed her. "We are not children, Elizabeth. There was no need to do something so extreme on our behalf. We can fend for ourselves!"

"Indeed we can," chimed in Aunt Louisa, agreeing with her sister for perhaps the first time in their adult lives. "To think that you would put yourself at risk of marriage to a man you abhor, just for us—it defies imagination!"

Elizabeth felt a rush of affection for her two dotty, beloved aunts.

"I thought my ruse had worked, until Victor scooped me up from Chapel Street," Elizabeth continued, her voice rueful. "I do not think I realized how desperate he was until he did that. I became desperate myself. I ran away, and that is how I came to fall into Lord Langdon's garden." She gave the assembled company a weak smile.

"What did Newfield intend that day?" Spencer's voice was sharp as he spoke from the position he had adopted, leaning against the fireplace mantel.

She turned to look at him, and her heart thudded into her rib cage. Just an hour ago, they had promised to be friends. But friendship was not what came to her mind as she gazed at him. Instead, she remembered the feeling of his arms, surprisingly strong, around her. She closed her eyes, reliving that extraordinary embrace in the kitchen. A sharp ache pierced her, an ache for something she had never realized she had missed.

He appeared a bit stiff, and she realized that his shoulders were probably in agony as he leaned against the hard marble. But she already knew him to be a man who would die rather than admit discomfort.

She forced her mind back to his question. "What did Victor intend? He intended to force me to the altar that very afternoon."

Across the room, Aunt Louisa gasped and raised a plump hand to her mouth. Aunt Harriet, bless her, spat out a salty phrase. Lady Riverton exclaimed, "How on earth did he intend to do that?"

"Victor never could keep a secret," Elizabeth said wryly. "As soon as he had me in the carriage, he began trying to impress me with the extent of his forethought. He had already bribed the vicar of St. Stephen the Martyr in Chelsea. He purposely picked a church of which I had never heard, and had procured a special license—although heaven only knows where he found the funds to do so. Everything was completely legal. He could tow me up the aisle on a rope, and no one—not the vicar, not his handpicked witnesses—would dare to protest."

"Good God." Spencer's voice was tight. "The man should be hanged."

"I would be satisfied if he would just leave me alone." Elizabeth sighed. "Truly, I do not know why he hates me so."

"Probably because you have managed your inheritance well, while he has squandered his." Spencer pushed himself away from the fireplace, with a tiny wince that Elizabeth suspected she was the only one to notice. "I must admit, I have no remorse about interfering in such an unholy betrothal."

So he had said in the kitchen. But she suspected his reasons then were somewhat less noble. She suppressed a grin.

Amid murmurs of agreement that Elizabeth was well within her rights to walk away from Victor, Aunt Louisa raised a troubled voice.

"I am horrified to think of all you have risked on our behalf," she cried. "Think of the stain on your reputation if this story ever becomes public! A woman who cries off once is forever tainted in the minds of potential suitors. This will place you forever on the shelf." She twisted her soft hands in her lap.

Impulsively, Elizabeth crossed the room and knelt before her elderly relative. "Please, Aunt Louisa, do not fret. If all goes as I have planned, no one need know that this 'betrothal' ever existed. And do you not think that my position as a businesswoman has already put me beyond the pale? Truly, I have never felt that marriage was for me. My life's work will be to maintain the business Father left me."

"But to what end? What use is it to build a thriving business if there are no children to inherit it?"

The shock that Aunt Louisa's question engendered in Elizabeth almost knocked her back on her heels. She had never once, in all her years of learning the business, and in the months since her parents had passed, given the slightest thought to the question her aunt had just posed. Roger Scott Importing was to be maintained for its own sake. That was the trust her father had given her. She had never debated the ultimate purpose of running the business. She had been too busy just getting through each busy day.

However, she needed to answer her aunt quickly, before this discussion degenerated into a conversation about her unnatural place in society. "Do not worry about that, Aunt Louisa," she said with a laugh. "I shall cross those bridges when I come to them." It was an inane response, but it was the best she could come up with in the circumstances.

"I appreciate your concern for Miss Scott's ultimate welfare, Mrs. Timms," Spencer chimed in from the other side of the room. "At the moment, however, we must focus on the immediate issue. Newfield is desperate. As a result, he will be back. And when he returns, I think Miss Scott and her aunts should be long gone from Linden Park."

Irrationally, Elizabeth longed to hear him call her by her Christian name again.

Stop behaving like a moonstruck schoolgirl, she chastised herself.

"That is a valid point," she began. *Spencer,* she added in her mind.

Why was she so distracted, in a matter of such vital import as this? She had never had trouble focusing on discussions of business, no matter what her personal troubles. Why was it so difficult to concentrate?

Perhaps because none of her business associates had even run his fingers through her undone hair.

"That is a valid point," she repeated, trying to marshal her faculties. "But where shall I go? I cannot go home—that is the first place Victor will look. And I cannot go to another of your estates," she added, with a quick smile at Lord Riverton, who had seemed about to propose just that.

"Your estates will be next on Victor's list, I am certain," she explained.

She returned to her seat beside Benjamin and settled back down into the comfortable wing chair. "I believe my next move," she concluded, "is to disappear quietly to a country inn of some sort, where my aunts and I can live in anonymity until Mr. Mason finishes consolidating my affairs."

"With all due respect, Miss Scott, I do not think that wise."

"And why is that, Mr. Willoughby?" Her voice was crisp. She had spent too long in a position of authority at Roger Scott Importers to be comfortable with constant contradiction of her suggestions—even from Spencer.

"Newfield may be having Linden Park watched. He obviously has a spy here, to have found you so quickly."

"It is not at all obvious. Gerald Reynolds let him know I was staying with your family. It was just a matter of time before he arrived here."

"He arrived far too quickly," Spencer countered. "Linden Park is the most distant of our estates from London. It would likely have been last on his list, not first or second."

"What else do you suggest, then, Mr. Willoughby?" Elizabeth gave him what she hoped was a quelling stare. It did not appear to affect him in the least degree.

"Lord and Lady Langdon are honeymooning at their estate in Oxfordshire," he began. "I propose that we decamp there, until the storm has passed."

"We?" Elizabeth's voice was incredulous. "Truly, Mr. Willoughby, I cannot impose on you or your family any longer. The incident this morning proves that I have overstayed my welcome. I shall depart, along with Aunt Louisa and Aunt Harriet, and leave you all to return to your normal lives—with my undying gratitude, of course."

"Miss Scott!" Spencer's voice was sharper than she had ever heard it. "Has nothing that has happened here— including today's unfortunate incident—convinced you that I and my family will not leave you to face your fate alone?"

"But I am not your responsibility! I am well used to fending for myself, and while I appreciate your kindness—"

"No. You will not reject my offer of help." Spencer crossed the room to stand before her. Once again, it felt as though they were the only two people in the room. "If you leave Linden Park without me, I will follow you and find you. You shall not escape, so it will be much easier to simply go along with my plan." He paused, then favored her with his most ingratiating smile. "Humor me, please. So few people do."

"I sincerely doubt that," Elizabeth replied, grinning in spite of herself.

"Humor me," he repeated, the intensity in his eyes reminiscent of the look he had given her just before he kissed her. She stared up at him, and her resolve faltered.

Would it be so wrong, she wondered, to stay in his company for a few more days? This strange interlude between them would end soon enough.

But would it? Could there be a future for them, together?

She had, after all, overcome her lifelong distrust of the aristocracy, Elizabeth thought. Aside from her family, she knew of no other person, noble or cit, who would have done as much on her behalf as had Spencer and his family.

And her earlier fears that he was a gambler had vanished, when she had learned that Spencer's pockets were to let for legitimate reasons that had nothing to do with wagering in gaming hells.

But, she reminded herself, marriage would likely mean giving up her business, her trust from her father, all that she had worked for.

And, she recalled with growing sadness, if Mr. Willoughby ever discovered she was not Roger Scott's true child, but instead a mere by-blow, what little interest he had in her would surely dissipate.

No, there was no possibility that their worlds could ever join.

So would it be so wrong to bask in his warm regard for just a few more days?

"Elizabeth, listen to sense." Aunt Harriet's blunt voice sliced into her thoughts. "The young gentleman is right. Victor is violent and desperate. You may run Roger Scott Importing and our home like clockwork, but Victor has already shown he can physically overpower you. If Mr. Willoughby is so kind as to offer you his protection, I think you should stop being stubborn and accept it, you silly chit." Pleased with her speech, Aunt Harriet leaned her angular body back into the cushions of the settee and crossed her arms across her bony chest.

Feeling like a naughty child caught raiding the larder, Elizabeth gave the assembled company a sheepish smile. Her aunt's words had tipped the balance. Elizabeth would continue this madness for a few more days, despite her misgivings.

"I'm afraid I have been less than gracious, Mr. Willoughby," she said, her gaze returning to him. "Please forgive me. I would be most grateful to accept your offer of assistance."

His grin lit up his entire face. "Well done, Miss Scott! I assure you, you shan't regret it."

Once more, he began to stroll around the room. "It will likely take us two days to reach Langdon Hall from here. Benjamin has already kindly agreed to accompany us." At this statement, Benjamin nodded and gave Elizabeth's hand a brotherly pat.

"Mr. Willoughby—" she said, turning to him. She was about to protest that Benjamin was needed on the estate, but Spencer cut her off.

"Remember, Miss Scott, you promised to be gracious."

She bit her tongue.

Seeing that she had silenced herself, he continued.

"We must leave with all haste, and I believe it would be wise to travel discreetly. This afternoon, Ben and I shall go to Stoke-on-Trent to let two plain black carriages. All of ours are emblazoned with the Riverton crest, making them a bit of a target."

"But why the need for such secrecy, Mr. Willoughby? As long as we make sure Mr. Newfield is nowhere about when we leave, will that not be enough?" Aunt Louisa's voice trembled with nerves.

"Did you not just hear the man say that Victor probably has a spy here somewhere? Honestly, Louisa, if you would only pay attention—"

Her aunts were back to their usual ways, Elizabeth thought with affectionate exasperation. She shouldn't have anticipated that any lull in their lifelong squabbling would last more than a few minutes.

"Miss Johnson is right," Spencer interjected. "I strongly believe Newfield has an entrée into Linden Park."

"But who?" Lady Riverton cried.

"It could be anyone," her youngest son replied. "I did not like the looks of that gentleman at dinner the other night, Mr. Roberts, for example. Being freshly arrived from Town, he may well have been one of Victor's associates."

Lady Riverton's face fell. "If that is the case, I do apologize, Miss Scott. 'Twas I who invited him and his sister, on a momentary whim."

"Do not trouble yourself," Elizabeth replied. "You could not have known."

"The identity of any informants Victor may have is not the point," Spencer said, returning doggedly to his plan. "The point is that we need to evade detection. That is why I propose that we escape Linden Park in disguise."

"Disguise!" Aunt Louisa exclaimed. "How exciting!"

Aunt Harriet shot her a scathing look.

"What sort of costume do you suggest, Mr. Willoughby?" Aunt Louisa burbled, ignoring her sister.

"The simplest may be the best," he replied. "I propose we make the journey dressed as members of the opposite sex."

A startled silence fell over the room. Then Benjamin Willoughby laughed.

"I know I agreed to this mad plan, Spence, but I'm not at all certain it will work. Miss Scott will be transformed into the shortest adult man in England, while I shall be a veritable Amazon!"

"The disguises need not be believable up close," Spencer explained. "They just need to fool someone looking at us in the early dawn light, at a distance. Anyone Victor has watching for us will be looking for three petite women, possibly accompanied by several men. If they see just two women leave—including one gargantuan one"—he grinned at his brother—"and realize that no one in the party matches our description, it may be enough to confuse them."

"I agree," Elizabeth announced, eager to support Spencer's idea in light of the others' rejection of it. "It is by the far the best disguise we could devise on such short notice. We must begin planning at once."

Twelve

The sharp morning air nipped at Elizabeth's ankles. She heartily wished she could fall asleep as easily as Aunt Louisa, who had dropped into slumber not ten minutes after they had clambered into the hired carriage in the dimness of dawn. But the chill dampness had chased away any thoughts of sleep for Elizabeth.

She supposed she felt the cold more keenly than usual because her legs were not swathed in yards of silk or wool, as was usually the case. Instead, they were encased in rather form-fitting pantaloons, unearthed from a trunk in a disused spare room. Lady Riverton, on producing them with a flourish, had guessed that they had once belonged to a teenaged Spencer.

The thought of wearing clothes that had once belonged to Spencer Willoughby gave Elizabeth an odd, undeniable thrill. The bulky topcoat she wore—purposely large to hide her giveaway curves—and the worn linen shirt below it had also come from Spencer's youthful wardrobe. She imagined him as he must have been then, all gangly limbs and winning smiles.

He was certainly not smiling now, she reflected as she glanced across the carriage. Spencer was staring out the window, tension evident in the stiffness of his arm on the window frame and the alert tilt of his head. One hand was poised next to the compartment where, earlier that morning, she had seen him hide a small traveling pistol.

His pose was hilariously at odds with the ensemble he wore. Aunt Louisa had taken one of her old dresses and lengthened it, using the ruffle from a torn evening gown of a similar olive shade that had once belonged to Lady Riverton.

Green was not his color. He looked positively sallow.

Of course, the large yellow poke bonnet didn't help matters. Although it did shield his face from the curious, it did nothing at all for his complexion.

Perhaps a green bow would help, Elizabeth thought, trying to imagine the effect. Suddenly cognizant of the trail her thoughts had taken, she laughed aloud.

Startled from his scrutiny of the passing scene, Spencer swiveled his gaze toward her. "Do share the joke, Elizabeth," he said.

Elizabeth cast a quick glance at her aunt, worried that her elderly relative might remark on Spencer's familiar use of her Christian name, but Aunt Louisa continued to snore gently.

"I've been staring at this monotonous verge for over an hour, looking for any sign of pursuit. If anyone had seen us leave, they would have caught us up long before now. As a result, I would heartily welcome a distraction," Spencer continued, turning away from the window. His hand, she noticed, remained close to the gun compartment.

"I do not think you shall welcome this one."

"Let me be the judge."

"I was just thinking," she paused to chuckle again, "that you would look much more fetching in robin's egg blue. It would bring out your eyes."

Spencer scowled. "You are right. I am heartily sorry I ever devised this idea of disguises. How do you women put up with all this fabric rustling about your knees? Makes it demmed hard to walk."

"I suppose you get used to it. I was just thinking that pantaloons are much less warm than skirts."

"But much more fetching." As Spencer turned fully from the window and glanced at her calves, she felt a blush rising to her cheeks.

She must not let this infatuation with Spencer Willoughby go any further than it should. There were many reasons that marriage was impossible for her, and many reasons that she would make a most unsuitable wife for him. Assuming, of course, that he would even offer for her.

"I wish I could say the same for you." This time her laughter erupted and she could not stop. Tears of mirth rolled down her warm cheeks.

Spencer pretended to bristle. "You mean that this ensemble is not in the highest stare of fashion? Why, I believe I saw one very much like it in the latest issue of *Le Beau Assemblé.*"

"You must mean *La Belle Assemblée.* Really, miss, you must make more of an effort to stay au courant."

Spencer chuckled. "I really am most woefully ill-informed. But do you not think I make a fine young lady nonetheless?" He batted his eyes at her in mock coquetry.

"You do not! Despite your formidable dramatic skills, there is not one person within a mile who could possibly mistake you for a woman."

It was true. While Benjamin, to no one's surprise, made a preposterous female, Aunt Louisa had commented to Elizabeth late the previous evening that she thought the younger Mr. Willoughby might make a tolerably believable lady, from a distance.

"After all, he is so fair and slim," she had argued.

Fair and slim he might be, Elizabeth conceded, but there was no mistaking that he was male, despite his purported disguise. She had watched him walking around the carriages this morning, getting things organized, making sure that trunks were strapped down safely and that everyone had what they needed for a comfortable journey. Something in the way he strode so purposefully, or perhaps in the set of his shoulders or the obstinate jut of his chin, would proclaim him a man no matter what he wore.

She sighed.

"Are you well, Elizabeth?" Spencer's voice was solicitous.

"Quite well, thank you," she said with a guilty start. Her thoughts had been moving once more in a perilous direction, and she welcomed the diversion.

"A bit fatigued, perhaps," she added. "I did not sleep well last night."

"Nor I," he admitted. "But soon we shall stop for something to eat. There is a pretty inn about a mile from here."

"It will be pleasant to stretch and move about," she replied, shifting in her seat. "My legs always become quite stiff on long carriage rides."

"Mmmm. Yes, I think it would be wise to stretch your legs," Spencer murmured, and she became aware that he was admiring her limbs once more.

"Really, Spencer, you must stop ogling me as though you had never seen a woman before. Otherwise, I shall have to call you out!" She laughed to cover up her mounting discomfort with his scrutiny.

"Perhaps I have not seen a woman before." His voice was playful.

"I doubt that." She was a little uncomfortable with the turn the conversation had taken, and yet she found herself most curious, suddenly, to learn more about the women Spencer had known.

"Do I appear such a libertine?"

"No, not at all. But you are certainly charming, and most women are a ready mark for charm."

"Ah, you know me too well, Elizabeth," he said.

"So?"

"So what?"

"So are you going to reveal to me the secrets of your past?" She smiled, as though encouraging a business rival to divulge information on his latest acquisitions.

Mr. Willoughby looked at Aunt Louisa and raised his eyebrows.

"You need not worry. She always sleeps as though she were drugged. She shall not hear a word of your long, sordid tale, I assure you."

Spencer hooted. "The tale is neither sordid nor long, I am afraid. I have had my share of rides in Hyde Park and dances at Almack's—along with a few nights at Vauxhall or Drury Lane in the company of various young ladies."

"Would those young ladies at Drury Lane be daughters of the Quality in your box—or engaging thespians you encountered after the performance?"

Spencer's jaw dropped in astonishment. "Really, Elizabeth, you ask the most direct questions!"

"I know it is impertinent, but I am curious. And how else am I to discover the information I seek, if I do not ask directly?" Elizabeth's nervous laugh betrayed her chagrin at her *faux pas*. But now that she had opened the discussion, she would not back down.

This time, Spencer did not merely hoot. His guffaw almost, but not quite, awakened Aunt Louisa. She snuffled, shifted her position against the door and emitted a soft snore.

"*Touché,* Elizabeth. You are quite right. I am just not used to such forthrightness in a woman."

"One would imagine you would have become somewhat accustomed to it after spending a few days in my company." She grinned, enjoying their verbal sparring match. "Now, come, Spencer, you are evading the question. I have spent more than a few nights at the theater myself, and I know that the leading actresses are often the toast of society. Have you ever been among the admiring young bucks gathered at the backstage door?"

"Perhaps, once or twice. When I have nothing else to amuse me."

"Ah, the truth comes out!" Elizabeth laughed.

"I did not wish to be deceptive. When I first came down from Oxford, having spent several years mainly in the company of obnoxious young men such as myself, my most fervent wish was to make the acquaintance of some lovely young women."

"Really?" She had little knowledge of what actually transpired behind the scenes at Drury Lane, although she had heard rumors from the brothers of school friends. Whatever it was, she was certain Spencer Willoughby would be in the midst of the activity, making sly comments and attracting the notice of the most popular actresses.

At the thought of him in the arms of another, she felt a cold stone of envy in the pit of her stomach.

Do not be foolish. You did not even know him then, and you have no claim upon him now. It would be unnatural if the man had been a monk.

"Yes. And that is all I shall say on that score. Honest I shall be, but I shall not play to your prurient interests." He wagged a mocking finger at her. "Truth be told, most nights in Town, I find myself at White's."

The mention of White's reminded Elizabeth of her early fears. "It is strange to recall now, but when first we met, I was convinced you were one of those men with an inordinate fondness for the gaming table," she confessed.

"I? A high-stakes gambler?" Amusement bubbled beneath his words.

She nodded.

"Why would you think that?"

The conversation about his amorous past had not embarrassed her unduly, but this topic did make her feel ashamed of herself. "Your mother and your brother both intimated that your pockets were to let," she mumbled, flushing. "In my experience, such a situation is often linked to gaming."

"Do not be embarrassed," Spencer replied, reaching out to squeeze her hand. His gentle touch brought sensations of their embrace in the kitchen rushing through her. She would give much to relive those few moments once again.

"It is understandable that you would be suspicious of a man whose money seemed to be disappearing without apparent reason," Spencer continued, oblivious to her woolgathering. "But you know my secret now."

"Your work in optics."

He nodded. "It is not a flamboyant way to run through an inheritance, but it appeals to me much more than does faro." He leaned back against the window, and flinched.

"Your back, Spencer! Do be careful. Are you in a great deal of pain?"

"I do like hearing you say my name." He smiled.

"Do not dodge the question."

"My back does smart, but they are only surface wounds. It is a mercy that I was wearing a heavy coat, due to the chill in the barn, so Victor's lashing did not do nearly the damage it could have done. I shall be right as rain in a few days, with a few more applications of your Aunt Louisa's salve."

"I am glad to hear it." A silence fell between them. Elizabeth wondered if he, like she, was recalling their moments in front of the kitchen fire.

Suddenly, the chill of the carriage had ceased to bother her.

She almost jumped when the Rivertons' coachman

rapped sharply on the roof. "I can see the village in the distance, sir," he called out. "We shall be there within ten minutes or so."

Gratefully, she leaned over to waken Aunt Louisa.

Elizabeth stood up from the table in the inn's private dining room. She felt much restored after a comforting lunch of roast beef and boiled potatoes.

Leaning down to Aunt Harriet, who was enjoying a last cup of strong tea, she whispered, "Before we move on, I shall just dash out to the necessary. Where did you find it, Aunt Harriet?"

"Just on the far side of the stable yard." Her aunt indicated the direction. "You will not linger there long, I can assure you. Louisa said it gave her the fright of her life."

"Was the stable yard as busy as it was when we arrived?"

"Even more so," her aunt replied. "It seemed half the population of the county was milling about there."

That was good. There was little chance that anyone could harm her there, in such a throng. Unlike Chapel Street, there would be many people about to witness anything that Victor—or his associates—might attempt.

"I shall be right back." Elizabeth slipped from the room.

Once outside, she quickly spotted the necessary, half enclosed by a thicket of thornbushes. She scooted into it.

Emerging minutes later from the rather dire facilities, she scanned the stable yard. Thankfully, this was a busy inn, and she had no fear being out here without a companion. She would have died rather than embarrass either Spencer or Benjamin by forcing them to accompany her, in their outlandish garb.

As she stepped away from the necessary, however, she felt an iron grip encircle her upper right arm. As she began to scream, a huge hand holding a foul-smelling rag clapped over her mouth and nose.

"Shut up, you stupid baggage." Victor's voice chilled her. "If you don't shut up, I swear, I shall drive a knife into you right here. Should have done that long ago. I would have, too, if I had thought I could get your money, without the bother of taking you along with it." He flung his arm across her chest to grip her left arm, yanking her roughly against him and immobilizing both her arms in the process.

Elizabeth struggled, but his grasp on her was tight. Memories of that day in Chapel Street came flooding back. She had struggled then, too, and had only succeeded when he had released his grip inside the carriage. She suspected he would not be so careless again.

"But this time you will not run away," he said as he dragged her back toward the thicket.

"You and your toffs think you are so much smarter than I," Victor muttered. "But it never occurred to you that I could bribe one of the Linden Park servants to feed me information." He gave a dry, mirthless laugh. "You probably did not even know that one of the stable hands resents the bloody Rivertons because he has not been raised yet to the position of groom."

A thorn scraped against her leg, and Elizabeth gasped in pain. As the nauseatingly sweet air coming through the rag flooded her throat, she spluttered.

"Take a deep breath, dear cousin." Victor continued to pull her back behind the necessary, far from the activity of the stable yard.

Wildly, she shook her head, trying to escape the wretched odor that was already overwhelming her nostrils. It must be some sort of drug. Already, her head was beginning to thrum in a most peculiar manner.

"You really did not think you would fool anyone in this idiotic costume?" Victor was asking. "Oh, a blind man, perhaps. But whatever else one can say about you, you are most inarguably a woman, and a particularly hard one to disguise, at that." His voice was laced with some emotion Elizabeth did not care to identify.

Think, Elizabeth, think! Recalling the fight in the barn yesterday, she remembered Victor's scream of pain when Spencer's chemicals had seared his leg. Kicking backward with all her strength, she clipped Victor on the right shin.

Victor swore and stumbled slightly, but did not release his hold. "You bloody baggage!"

She kicked again, but her legs felt numb, as though she was very cold. Come to think of it, she were very cold.

She stabbed her foot backward a third time, but did not connect with anything solid. She pitched forward, and only Victor's arm kept her from falling. She shivered.

Why was it so chilly when the sun was shining?

With that thought, she lost consciousness.

"Where is Miss Scott?" Spencer's voice, pitched low to avoid giving any passing servants from the inn a clue to Elizabeth's real identity, was urgent. Deep in conversation with a coachman about the best route to Matthew's estate, he had not noticed her slip from the room.

"She left to use the necessary." Harriet Johnson's voice was equally low, more due to embarrassment at discussing such things with a man than to any sense of discretion, he suspected.

"When?" he barked.

Miss Johnson looked flustered. "I am not sure. Just after she left, the innkeeper asked if we should like some cheese, and I was discussing it with him—" She broke off and scratched her head. "Perhaps ten minutes ago."

"And she left the room alone?" Spencer struggled to keep the rising fear out of his voice.

Apparently he failed, as Elizabeth's aunt's voice was uncharacteristically anxious as she replied. "I thought it no harm. The necessary is in the stable yard, and there are many people about. She assured me she would return immediately."

Spencer scanned the room, as if by some miracle Elizabeth would be hiding behind one of the faded velvet curtains or in the cubbyhole beside the massive wooden sideboard. She was not.

Lunging across the room, he paused only to grab Benjamin's arm and haul him out the door behind him.

Together, the brothers scanned the yard, but saw no sign of Miss Scott. Spencer even yanked open the door of the filthy necessary, damning propriety, but the wretched chamber was empty. As he strode behind it, however, he saw a small scrap of buff-colored cloth hanging from a thornbush.

The pantaloons Miss Scott had borrowed were made of that fabric.

Raw, cold fury seized him by the throat.

He ran back toward the stable yard and beckoned to his brother, wordlessly showing him the scrap.

"I'll question the people in the yard. You try to find out whether anyone in the inn saw anything untoward," he shouted over his shoulder. For once, Benjamin obeyed him without debate.

Ten minutes later, Spencer was almost frantic with frustration. Several people remembered seeing a slight young man wearing an odd hat and buff pantaloons, but no one recalled where the man had gone. Finally, just before he turned toward the inn to join Benjamin inside, he felt a tug on his skirts.

Surprised, he looked down to see a small girl of about eight.

"Are you looking for the drunk man, miss?"

The drunk man? Possibly. He nodded.

"I saw him."

"Where?" He tried to pitch his voice high, hoping to fool the child so that she wouldn't be distracted by his ridiculous clothes.

"I was coming out to use the necessary . . ." She hesitated.

"It is all right," he encouraged her, clenching his teeth to control his impatience. "What did you see?"

"I saw a tall man holding the little man up. He had a handkerchief over the little man's face. I guessed the little man was going to be sick. He was stumbling, like my papa does sometimes when he comes home from the pub."

"What was the little man wearing?"

"I'm not sure. A big coat, I remember that." She chewed her lower lip. "And a funny hat! Like old people wear. It almost fell off his head when he stumbled."

It sounded as though she had been drugged.

"And the big man? Was he bigger than me?"

The little girl nodded. "He had black hair. He called the little man a baggage."

Victor.

Spencer knelt down so that he was eye to eye with the child. "Did you see where they went?"

The girl smiled. "You aren't a lady at all! You're a man dressed up as a lady!"

Spencer gave her a quick smile. "I am on my way to a masquerade. But first, I must find my friend, the drunk man. Did you see where he went?"

"The big man pulled him over to a blue carriage. I remember the carriage, because it had two pretty brown horses."

Spencer looked wildly about the yard, but of course the carriage was gone.

"Thank you," he shouted to the child as he dashed back to the inn.

Ten minutes later, clad in his own clothes once more, Spencer was clattering across the cobbled yard on a hired horse. Benjamin had offered to accompany him, but he had convinced his older brother to continue with Elizabeth's aunts to Langdon Hall.

"Who knows how many bloody accomplices Victor has hiding in the woods?" he'd spat as he'd pulled on his boots. "The man's deranged. He could have Elizabeth's family taken hostage, or God knows what. I'll continue on to London, and join you at Langdon Hall as soon as I have found Elizabeth."

"How do you propose to find her, Spence? London is not exactly a country village, you know."

"I will find her," he had replied as he'd hurtled from the room.

As the dirt of the country road flew by below his heels, Spencer reflected that he had a very good idea where Victor Newfield had taken Elizabeth. The only trick would be finding the church of St. Stephen the Martyr in the unfamiliar streets of Chelsea.

He scanned the landscape to the horizon but saw no sign of a blue carriage pulled by two chestnut horses. If Victor had taken this road, Spencer had a good chance of overtaking him. Although Newfield had a good twenty-minute lead on him, Spencer's horse—a rather fine specimen for an animal hired from a country inn—would easily be able to outpace a carriage.

Unfortunately, the inn was located at the intersection of a number of roads, several of which could be used to travel to London. Spencer had chosen the quickest route, but Victor could have selected a more roundabout way to reach the capital, in the hopes of avoiding detection.

After an hour in hot pursuit, Spencer became resigned to the fact that he would likely not encounter Victor's carriage on the road. He would have to content himself with catching the scoundrel red-handed at St. Stephen the Martyr.

But what if Victor took her to another church? Or came up with an alternate plan altogether?

Another dire thought pierced Spencer's brain as his horse's hooves thundered along the road below. In his rush to leave the inn, he had left his traveling pistol behind in the rented carriage.

Damn! he cursed silently. His odds were long enough as it was, without leaving himself unarmed in the bargain.

Spencer tamped down such thoughts and spurred his horse on toward London. In his rage, he barely noticed his throbbing shoulders.

Thirteen

Elizabeth tried once more to clear her mind. Her head felt as though it had been stuffed with wet cotton, then filled with quarreling bees. Some of those bees had migrated to her stomach, as well. She would not be at all surprised if she cast up her accounts all over the flagstone floor.

Mustn't do that. Would be sacrilegious in a church.

Elizabeth glanced to her right, catching a glimpse of Victor's tense profile before a wave of nausea engulfed her. Losing her equilibrium, she pitched forward slightly, until her cousin's iron grip on her elbow yanked her upright.

"Do not even think about running off again, you tiresome chit," he hissed.

Running? She could barely stand upright.

Slowly, so as not to trigger her rebellious stomach into action once more, Elizabeth looked around the small, dim church. It was empty save for herself, Victor, Gerald Reynolds, and a fourth man sprawled in a front pew.

The unknown man caught her eye and leered.

Who was he? Why did he look so familiar?

Elizabeth cursed herself. She usually had an excellent memory for faces, and she was certain she had met this man only days before.

"It ain't exactly the drawing room at Linden Park, is it, *Lady Mary?*" he drawled.

Mr. Roberts. Of course. The dinner guest who had so roused Spencer's suspicions. It must have been he who had made Victor aware of her location.

Again, Elizabeth berated herself. She must not allow herself to become distracted. If she did not start trying to solve the problem at hand, she would certainly be leg-shackled within the hour.

"Where is that demmed priest?" Victor shouted. "Roberts, you did tell him we were coming?"

"Yes, told him yesterday. He will be here. We are early, you know." Mr. Roberts flicked a bit of lint from his rather threadbare brown jacket.

"The earlier we get started, the earlier this business will be done." Victor motioned to Elizabeth's faithless manager. "Reynolds, make yourself useful. Go see if you can find the man."

Gerald heaved himself up from the pew and ambled toward the vestry. Elizabeth noted that he made elaborate efforts to avoid looking her in the eye.

As well he should. If she managed to escape this crisis in full possession of her sanity, she fully intended to give Gerald a tongue-lashing such as he would never forget.

Just before she sent him away without a reference.

Escape this crisis. That was the matter at hand. Why could she not focus? Elizabeth took a deep breath, and decided that the first task should be to extricate her hands. Someone—Victor, she supposed—had bound her wrists with rough twine, before thrusting a huge bouquet between her clenched palms. Some trailing strands of ivy easily hid the twine.

For all the world, she looked like a blushing bride.

Victor had even procured a rather ill-fitting dress of rose silk. At the thought that it must have been he—or one of his minions—who had put it on her, Elizabeth almost reeled from nausea again. Fearful of incurring Victor's wrath again, she forced her knees to stay steady.

Tentatively, she twisted her left wrist, gritting her teeth as the twine scraped her skin. It was as tight as a band of iron. She twitched her wrist again.

Victor shook her elbow. "Did I not just tell you not to try anything, you stupid baggage? I am standing right here, and I am not about to let you get away again."

Elizabeth stilled her hands.

There must be some other way.

She remembered Tony had once been in a fight down on the docks with a cutpurse. When she asked him how he had escaped, he had grinned and mentioned something about kneeing the bigger man in the groin. Then, of course, he had realized he should not be sharing such knowledge with his little sister, and promptly apologized.

Elizabeth wondered how much force one would have to use in such a maneuver. Now that Gerald was gone, if she could incapacitate Victor, she would need only to evade William Roberts and she could be free. It would be awkward running with her hands tied, but she would never have a better opportunity.

What did she have to lose?

Praying her stomach would not betray her, she spun quickly on her right heel while raising her left knee. Fortunately, the silk dress had rather capacious skirts. With all the force she could muster, she slammed her knee into Victor . . . and hit him squarely on the thigh.

"You bloody baggage!" Victor swore, clenching his thigh with his free hand. "You are the devil's own! When we are wed, I will make you sorry you were ever born."

Elizabeth felt the color drain from her face at this remark, recalling his vicious attack on Spencer in the barn.

He gripped her by both forearms. "Listen to me. We will be wed. I will have your money. It should have been mine in any case. Your cuckolded father was a fool to give it to a woman who was not even of his own blood."

Fury finally shocked Elizabeth from her muteness. "Do not defame my parents in this house of God."

"It is not defamation to speak the truth. Even the courts would hold it so." Victor's sneer sent a chill straight to Elizabeth's toes.

"If you wish to carry on the business of Roger Scott Importing, you might care to keep such information to yourself," Elizabeth replied. "No one likes dealing with a business tainted by scandal." She fought the revulsion that bubbled into her brain, and lost. "Or perhaps you plan to run that business into ruin as well? That, at least, is something you are good at."

He shook her again. "For the love of God, woman, do not . . ."

"Newfield!" Gerald Reynolds's tremulous voice wafted across the church's deserted pews. "I have found the vicar."

Despair washed over Elizabeth. Now she was outnumbered four to one. What could she possibly do to escape?

As Victor shoved her back into place beside him, so that they were demurely standing before the altar in a mockery of a bridal couple, she lowered her face into the bouquet so that he would not see the hot tears cascading down her face.

And then she sneezed.

Wishing desperately for a handkerchief, she made heroic efforts not to sniffle. The last thing she wanted was to draw Victor's attention to her in any way.

She sneezed again.

Stop it! she pleaded with her uncooperative body.

I must be getting a cold, she thought, as she looked up to see Victor frowning at her. However, she did not feel feverish, and her chest was not at all congested.

A third sneeze shook her from top to toe.

Elizabeth wondered what on earth was the matter with her. Then, with growing hopefulness, she looked more closely at the enormous but ragged bouquet Victor had obtained from a street-corner flower girl.

Among the carnations, daisies, and roses, she spotted a small cluster of lavender. Since childhood, lavender had made her sneeze uncontrollably.

This knowledge was not much, but perhaps she could use it to delay the proceedings somewhat. With luck, she could delay them until her drug-addled mind cleared, and she could think of a way out of this dilemma.

The vicar, a middle-aged gentleman with sad, tired eyes, took his place before the motley assembly. She almost felt sorry for him, until she remembered that he had taken a bribe to perform this most unorthodox ceremony.

"Dearly beloved, we are gathered together here . . ." he began in a sonorous monotone.

At the familiar words of the Book of Common Prayer wedding ceremony, Elizabeth felt a cold, clammy sweat dampening her forehead and clinging to her aching palms. It had begun. If she did nothing, she would soon be tied irrevocably to Victor Newfield.

She reached out one slippered foot, beneath her skirts, and kicked Victor in the shin.

"Ow!" he howled, before clamping a hand over his mouth. The other hand retained its grip on her elbow.

The priest glared at them.

"Nothing to worry about, Reverend." Victor put on his most ingratiating smile. "Old school injury. Acts up when I stand for any length of time."

The priest lowered his eyes to his prayerbook again.

Victor twisted his hand on Elizabeth's elbow. A whip of pain streaked up her arm, and her stomach turned over.

". . . gathered together here in the sight of God, and in the face of this congregation . . ."

Do two witless witnesses count as a congregation?
Elizabeth wondered.

For the love of God, woman, focus, she told herself.
Do something!

Desperate, she thrust her nose back into the bouquet.
The familiar tickle teased her nostrils. She breathed
deeply, and ran her tongue over the soft palate at the
back of her mouth.

She sneezed violently, blowing a small flutter of petals
onto the church floor.

The priest stopped his monologue, giving her time to
gather herself together.

Elizabeth smiled in what she hoped was an apologetic
manner. "I'm sorry, Reverend."

"No matter, no matter." He returned his glance to his
book. "Where was I? Oh yes, here we are . . . in the
sight of God, and in the face of this congregation . . ."

Beside her, she felt rather than heard Victor's groan
of frustration.

She allowed the priest to continue for a few seconds
more, than took another deep breath of the bouquet.

"Aaaaa-choooo!"

The priest stopped again.

"You vicious baggage! Stop this at once!" Victor released his grip on her elbow and raised his hand toward
her.

Sensing her last chance, Elizabeth stamped on Victor's
foot as hard as she could, then spun toward the door.
Before she had taken two steps, however, the door was
thrown back upon its hinges. A figure stood there, sil-
houetted against the bright afternoon sunlight. She
blinked, trying to see who it was. Before her eyes had
adjusted, however, the person spoke.

"Have you reached the part where you ask whether
'any man do allege and declare any impediment, why
they may not be coupled together in matrimony'?" she

heard Spencer Willoughby inquire in a conversational tone as the door slammed shut behind him.

Relief washed over her in an all-consuming wave, to be replaced almost immediately by terror. They were still vastly outnumbered, and Victor was in a black mood. Spencer should not have come here. She had put him in danger yet again. Rooted to the spot, she simply stared at him.

The priest, apparently also transfixed by the apparition at the back of the church, replied warily, "No, I have not."

"Well, then, let me save you the trouble." Spencer strolled up the aisle toward the unholy wedding party. Only the crease of tension across his forehead revealed that he was not completely at his ease in this bizarre situation. "I should like to allege and declare an impediment."

"And what would that impediment be?" The priest, probably foreseeing the loss of his plump bribe, spoke in a belligerent tone.

"Well, let me see. There is kidnapping, of course. And forcible confinement. And then, the bride's complete unwillingness to participate in the ceremony." He ticked each reason off on his fingers as he enunciated it. "Is that enough?"

Victor's hand shot out to clench Elizabeth's bound wrists. She stifled a cry of pain.

"Forget it, Willoughby. The priest is bribed and I have a special license. This wedding will take place, and it is legal."

"I shall have it challenged in court." Spencer continued his steady pace up the aisle.

"Ah yes, your fondness for running to the law. It shall do you no good this time. You shall not be here to launch any sort of suit." With his free hand, Victor reached into his coat pocket and extracted a pistol. He pointed it at Spencer's heart.

An earthquake of fear shuddered through Spencer's body as he eyed the gun. He knew that Victor would not hesitate to use it. The mania of desperation shone in the other man's eyes.

Spencer thought it ironic that he should have been thwarted from joining the army, thus avoiding the battlefields of Salamanca, only to die on the cold floor of a London church.

He forced himself to keep a steady eye on Newfield, and to keep his voice low and measured. He had been running from fear all his life. Today, if he was about to die, he would do it like a man.

Today, there was a cause worth risking his life for. He stole a look at Elizabeth. Her face was ashen, her mouth formed into a small, terrified O.

He could do this. For Elizabeth, he could do this.

"You do not want to shoot me, Newfield," he murmured, keeping his gaze firmly on Victor. "There are witnesses here. You will be clapped in jail just as surely as you would be for debt. You will be no further ahead."

"I will be no further behind, either!" Victor roared. "I am going to Fleet Prison any day now if I do not pay off my debtors. I will do anything to get this lying chit's money! Anything, do you hear me?"

"You will never get my money!" Elizabeth cried. "By now, Mr. Mason has probably succeeded in completely protecting my fortune."

In another life, Elizabeth could have been a formidable card player, Spencer thought. She was an excellent bluffer. Mason was at least a week away from completing his work.

"You will not see one penny, Victor!" she was shouting. "Not if you marry me. Not even if you . . . not even if you shoot Mr. Willoughby. So stop it, Victor. Give up this madness. It is all fruitless."

"You have taken legal means to protect your inheritance?" Victor twisted to face Elizabeth. "Your money is safe?"

"Safe as England's laws can make it." Her smile was triumphant.

"Then there is no reason why I should not kill you now as well, is there? You have been the bane of my existence since the day you were born. Willoughby is just in my way. But you. It would be worth going to prison to kill you." He slowly raised the gun toward Elizabeth's head.

From the moment Victor pointed the pistol at Elizabeth, Spencer saw the sanctuary through a red, pulsating haze. Like a runaway horse, he thundered up the aisle and, with one unerring movement, knocked the pistol from Victor's trembling hand. It clattered to the flagstones.

Howling in pain, Victor turned on him. Before the other man could say a word, however, Spencer sliced his jaw with a quick upper cut. Victor reeled backward, lost his footing, and crashed to the floor. His head hit the flagstones with a sickening thud. Then he was still.

From the corner of his eye, Spencer saw William Roberts advancing on him from the front pew. As the man approached, however, he suddenly stumbled. Looking for the impediment that had caused his fall, Spencer spotted Elizabeth's small foot in the aisle.

Quickly, he caught her eye and was astonished to see her flash him a quick grin. She had cast aside her bouquet, and he noticed that her hands were bound with coarse twine.

Before Roberts could regain his feet, Spencer dropped to the ground and retrieved Newfield's pistol. Rising, he cocked the hammer and turned the gun on Roberts.

"I would stay right there, if I were you," Spencer said. "This is Newfield's cause, not yours. Is it worth dying for?"

From his inelegant position on the floor, Roberts shook his head.

"How about you, Reynolds? Are you ready to die for Newfield?" Spencer turned to the pew where Elizabeth's manager had been sitting, but it was empty. The clatter of footsteps in the direction of the vestry revealed Reynolds's escape route.

"We do not want any shooting here, sir," the priest piped up in an aggrieved voice. "This is a house of worship, not some Whitechapel alley!"

"I would be most pleased to accommodate you, Reverend." Spencer's voice was dry. "Come, Elizabeth, I believe we are no longer needed here."

Slowly, she walked toward him, her steps uneven. With a pang, he realized she was still under the influence of the drug Victor had administered. The fact that her hands were still bound was probably not helping her balance, either. As she reached his side, he put his arm around her waist and drew her gently toward him, supporting her weight against him.

Keeping the pistol trained on the two supine forms on the church floor, he backed slowly up the aisle, steadying Elizabeth as they went. At the back of the church, he reached carefully behind him, twisted the doorknob open, and released them both into the clean, cool light of the spring afternoon.

Fourteen

Elizabeth glanced out the window of the creaking, hired carriage as the last vestiges of London slipped past. Ahead lay only blissful, open countryside. It looked fresh and clean. She felt the ugliness of the episode in St. Stephen the Martyr slipping from her, like dirt washed off her skin.

"Do you think we should have donned our disguises?" Spencer's amused voice broke into her reverie.

"As they worked so well the last time?" she replied with a grin.

"I must admit, I am not surprised Victor spotted you. Despite my best schoolboy coat, anyone would need to be blind to mistake you for a man." His voice was warm as his gaze took her in.

Despite her weariness and her still-throbbing head, Elizabeth felt a surge of pleasure engulf her. She might look like an antidote, clad as she was in the ill-fitting, out-of-date gown Victor had procured, but Spencer appeared to think her still worth a glance.

"It is a case of the pot calling the kettle black, Spencer." Calling him by his Christian name still felt delightfully illicit. "I do not imagine many were fooled by your ensemble."

She certainly had not been. A warm flush suffused her cheeks. As she'd watched him striding through the inn in his outrageous rig, an old shawl belonging to his mother draped awkwardly around his shoulders, all she had been able to think about was how magnificent those shoulders had appeared in the firelight of the Linden Park kitchen.

"You do not think I made a convincing young lady?" He batted his eyelashes—which, she had to admit, were outrageously long for a man's—and gave a weak approximation of a feminine giggle. "I do try to maintain an air of feminine decorum at all times," he said in a high falsetto.

She burst out laughing and he joined in. Goodness, it was lovely to be back in his company and far, far from Victor. Improper, certainly, to be traveling with him unescorted, but there was no help for that.

"I suppose we are best off playing the roles we were born to play," she conceded.

How true that was. Soon, she would return to her world in the City, and he would return to his at Linden Park. They would never have met had she not tumbled into Lord Langdon's garden, and it was unlikely they would ever meet again. She sighed.

"What troubles you?" His voice was rich with sudden concern, a concern that cut her to the quick. The steadfast interest in her welfare he had shown since first they met was the thing she would miss most of all about this exotic interlude in her life.

"Just thinking about Victor," she replied, coming up with the first plausible excuse she could think of for her sudden melancholy. She certainly could not tell him the real cause. There was no point. Once Mr. Mason had finished with her legal affairs, there would be no reason for her to stay with the Rivertons.

"We are free of him—for now," Spencer replied with a grin. He looked most pleased with himself, as well he should, she thought. He had bested four men, one armed and almost half again his size.

"I must thank you again for all your help on my behalf," she began, but Spencer waved her gratitude away.

"It was nothing, truly," he said. "It was about time I did something useful with myself, anyway."

"You must not talk so!" she cried. "Your work with optics . . ."

". . . is progressing with infinite slowness," he finished before she could say more. "But let us not talk of that for now. There is something I must broach with you." His mouth set itself into an uncharacteristically serious line.

"This sounds dire."

"It is not dire, but it is important." Spencer turned to face her more directly, wincing as he did so.

"Your back must still ache," she said, as concern lanced through her. "You must be in agony, with all this running about the countryside on my behalf . . ."

"Elizabeth, please!" His plea rang loudly in the small carriage.

She subsided, wondering what could have altered his bantering manner so quickly.

He took a deep breath. "Elizabeth." He stopped.

She remained silent, giving him time to continue.

The silence in the carriage grew.

"Elizabeth," he began again. "I would like to . . . I have long been thinking . . ."

Silence descended again. She longed to pull the words out of him, whatever he was trying to say. She had never seen charming, witty Spencer so speechless.

"Elizabeth, I would be most honored if you would consent to be my wife." The words came in a heedless rush, as though he was afraid he would not make it to the end of the sentence if he did not hurry.

Astonished, she stared at his dear face across the small space separating them. His wide blue eyes were as intent as she had seen them only once before—in that bewitching kitchen a few days previously, when he had kissed her.

Whatever she had been expecting him to say, it was not this. When he had been so eager to accept her solution to their possible compromise in the kitchen, she had acknowledged that he had no desire to wed a cit such as she. Secretly, she had been grateful, for it had saved her from having to reveal her even more humble origins as a nobleman's by-blow.

But part of her had not been grateful at all.

As his gaze continued to bore into hers, she knew she had to reply. And yet, what was she to say? Could she truly grasp this unexpected offer of happiness? Would he accept her, once he knew of her origins?

"But I am not fit," she began. "My family, there is a secret—"

He brushed her concerns away. "If we marry quickly, you will be completely protected from Victor." He grasped her right hand in both of his. "Until Mr. Mason has finished his work, there is every chance that Newfield will return. And this time, we may not be lucky enough to evade him."

As quickly as it had come, her euphoria drained away. He did not want to marry her. She had been a fool to even imagine it to be true. He was simply being chivalrous.

A cold, dull ache settled between her shoulder blades.

In the last few days, she had dared to believe that all his heroic efforts on her behalf had been motivated by admiration, respect, perhaps even love. But in his offer, he had not breathed one word of affection.

And now, she suddenly realized, affection—love—was what she craved most in the world. In particular, she wanted Spencer to love her. He was the only man who had ever elicited such hopes in her.

In growing panic, she realized that she loved him as

she would likely never love another man. They had already been through so much together.

And he, apparently—despite his kisses, despite his obvious enjoyment of her company—felt only the need to protect her. "You are very kind," she told him, withdrawing her hand from his. "But you have done far too much for me already. I cannot allow you to mortgage your entire life as well."

"Elizabeth, please do not speak so! I would be pleased to do it." He paused, seemed to consider adding something, then shook his head.

She could hear the axle of the carriage creaking and the soft clopping of the horses' hooves on the dirt road. She could hear her own quick breathing.

But she had not heard what she most wanted to hear. If he loved her at all, he would have said so by now.

Elizabeth's despair was so all-encompassing, it was as though she could feel it on her skin, taste it in her mouth, smell it in the air. It wrapped around her like a wet, cold shroud.

How could he hurt her this way?

She would not show him how much his practical proposal had cut her to the quick. If she did, she would break down.

"My fortune will soon be beyond anyone's reach but my own, Mr. Willoughby," she replied, her voice frosty. "You need not worry yourself about it." She inched away from him, toward the end of the seat.

His eyes narrowed, and an uncharacteristic scowl creased his forehead.

"Aside from protecting your money, there is no reason you would consider marrying me?" His voice was quiet.

Oh, so many, if only he loved her, and did not simply feel compelled to help her. She must be quick, and nip this entire idea in the bud. She could not bear to marry him if he did not love her, no matter how appealing the idea of marriage to him might be.

And it was very appealing.

She thought about asking him outright: "Do you love me?" But the question sounded so weak, so pathetic. And when he said "No," as she suspected he would, how would she ever look him in the eye again?

"There is no reason I can see why we should marry," she finally forced herself to say, the lie sticking in her throat like a fish bone.

He stared at her with unnerving attention for several seconds. She willed herself not to take her refusal back, as his face contracted with pain. Whether it was pain from his back, or from the thwarting of his desire to help her, she hated to cause him any distress.

But she had to do it.

Spencer folded his arms across his chest, and said nothing for what seemed like hours but was in reality probably only a minute. "Very well, then, Miss Scott," he said, in a voice more remote than any she had ever heard him use. "I am sorry to have distressed you." With that, he turned from her and looked out the window at the passing scene that had given her such joy and relief only a few minutes ago.

Her mind vacillating between anger and despair, Elizabeth turned from him as well, and stared unseeingly at the farmers' fields beyond the road's edge.

Elizabeth looked around the drawing room at Langdon Hall and gave a heartfelt, if inward, sigh. Yet again, a bevy of concerned people had gathered to discuss her life in excruciating detail. She was most grateful for their concern, but she was thoroughly sick of being in need of assistance. She was not used to relying so much on others, and the need to do so had become like an irritating itch she longed to scratch or salve.

The fact that she was once again watching Spencer pace across a carpet, his brow furrowed in thought, was not improving her mood, either. At the moment, he was explaining their escape from Victor to Aunt Louisa, Aunt Harriet, Benjamin, and Lord and Lady Langdon.

Why did Spencer not simply return to Linden Park and leave her here? She had told him she would not marry him. Victor could not possibly find her. So why was he continuing to take such an interest in her welfare? Could he not just go, and leave her in peace to forget about him? In a few days, she could return to London—back to her business, and back to a life free of the distraction of Mr. Spencer Willoughby.

He brushed a stray lock of hair out of his eyes, a gesture she had seen him make countless times. This time, however, the movement made her heart twist in regret. How she would have loved to have spent the rest of her life watching him. If only she could have said yes.

This time, she did sigh aloud, prompting a glance of concern from Aunt Harriet. Quickly, she shook her head, and her aunt returned her attention to Spencer.

Stop being a green girl, she admonished herself. Her decision had been the correct one. She had to stop woolgathering about a life that would not be.

With the determination for which she was famous in the City, she forced herself to concentrate on Spencer's tale.

It seemed, however, that he had finished describing their flight and had moved on to leading a discussion of the options for silencing Victor once and for all.

"Why can we not simply pay the scoundrel's debts?" asked Benjamin. "If he was no longer impoverished, he would have no reason to continue to annoy Miss Scott."

"No, Mr. Willoughby," she cried. "Victor does not

deserve one cent of my money—or yours. If we give him money, he shall have bested us."

"I agree," Spencer said. "That is why I am proposing to return to London to have a small discussion with Newfield."

"Forgive me, Mr. Willoughby," Elizabeth interjected. "But I do not see that any additional action is necessary. Victor cannot find me here, and soon my estate will be protected."

"So you have told me," he remarked in a curt voice.

She ignored his sarcasm. "With Lord and Lady Langdon's kind permission, may I not simply remain here for several days until my affairs are in order, and then return quietly to London?"

Spencer glanced at her, an unreadable look in his eyes. "No, Miss Scott, I feel that that would be most unwise. You saw Newfield's mania in the church. This is a matter that has gone far beyond money, I fear. He is furious with you, and I am convinced that he will spare no effort to punish you for your intransigence."

"Punish me?" Elizabeth loathed the note of panic that crept into her voice.

"Yes." He looked at her with an intensity that reminded her of their uncomfortable encounter in the carriage. Then, he turned away. "Victor was not afraid to hold a pistol to your head yesterday."

Although Spencer had related this part of the story before, Aunt Louisa gave a small gasp.

"As he himself pointed out, he has little to lose by harming you," Spencer continued. "Eventually, he will likely end up in prison anyway."

"Well, if he is in prison, he poses no harm to me. And, from what he said, it appears his imprisonment is imminent." Elizabeth was pleased to dismiss the disturbing thought of Victor coming back to do her harm.

"It is indeed. While I was in London meeting with

my investor, I also had the chance to speak with one of Newfield's creditors, Mr. Cox. He is on the verge of having Newfield charged with assault and arrested for debt." Briefly, Spencer outlined the details of his conversation with Henry Cox.

Elizabeth was astonished. "Why did you not share this information with me before?"

A brief look of what Elizabeth might once have taken for tenderness flashed through Spencer's eyes. "I did not want to give you even more cause to fear Victor than you already had."

Ah, yes, always solicitous for my welfare. Like a brother, Elizabeth thought sadly. Out loud, she observed, "Victor may be headed for prison even as we speak. As a result, I am out of harm's way."

"Not entirely. He could likely convince any of those thugs who surround him to finish the task."

Elizabeth felt a chill steal across her, as the truth of Spencer's argument sank in. She had no doubt that the cold-eyed Mr. Roberts, for one, would not hesitate to do her harm. He had no personal complaint against her, but she sensed he was a man who would actually find such a distasteful endeavor enjoyable for its own sake.

"I shall call in the law," she announced. "There is no need for us to deal any longer with Victor directly. Is that not what the courts are for?"

"The courts and the Bow Street Runners may be able to quell Victor, but his resentment toward you shall not dissipate. We need to devise a way to make certain that harming you is not in any way worth his while."

Elizabeth mulled this over. "Well, the one emotion in Victor that may be stronger even than hatred is his fear of embarrassment."

"Oh yes, he detests looking the fool," Aunt Louisa chimed in. "Do you remember that picnic we all went on at the Royal Botanic Gardens, when you children were small, Elizabeth?" Her aunt chuckled at the memory. "Victor chased a rabbit across the park, tripped, and fell headfirst into a pond. When he emerged, covered in mud and reeds, we all fell about laughing. Even then, as a small boy, he was furious with us for our amusement. I remember he went and sulked in the carriage. Wouldn't even come out for his tea.

"Of course, any child being laughed at would do that," she added. "But he remarked on that incident for years. I remember his mentioning it to your father not that long ago. He seemed to have taken it much too strongly to heart."

Spencer nodded. "You had apprised me earlier of Newfield's pride," he said to Elizabeth. "And that is why I think we must threaten him with embarrassment to make sure that he no longer poses a risk to you."

"What sort of embarrassment?" Despite herself, Elizabeth's curiosity got the better of her.

"I have given this a great deal of thought, and this is the solution I propose." Spencer stopped pacing back and forth before the fire and launched a slow stroll around the room, instead.

"Do you remember John Davis?" he asked Lord Langdon.

Langdon, who was sitting next to his wife on a small green settle, smiled. "Certainly I do. He blazed quite a trail through Oxford when we were there," he explained to Lady Langdon. "Was almost sent down several times for drunkenness, as I recall."

"The very man," Spencer replied. "Did you know that he is now the proprietor of the *Evening Record-Gazette*?"

"Yes. He wrote up a scathing indictment of Lord Stowcroft's opposition to my proposed poor relief measures. I read every glorious word."

"I believe John might be more than slightly interested

to hear of a prominent City merchant who is so lacking for female companionship that he has been reduced to blackmailing his own second cousin to secure a bride," Spencer replied, an evil glint sparkling in his blue eyes.

Despite herself, Elizabeth grinned. "Particularly if that merchant was also rumored to be on the verge of heading to debtors' prison." Abruptly, she stopped smiling. "But see, we are back to our problem, again. If Victor is about to be publicly embarrassed as a debtor, how will threatening to expose him as a blackmailer be any additional incentive to leave me alone?"

"Ah, yes. There is the whip, and then there is the carrot." Spencer was now directly behind Elizabeth's chair. She twisted around to gaze up at him.

"Please do not speak in code, Mr. Willoughby," she said. "What do you mean?"

"What I mean is that, in exchange for promising not to expose Mr. Newfield as a blackmailer, I shall make it possible for him to escape his creditors and the public embarrassment of debtors' prison."

"How shall you do that, short of giving him money?" Elizabeth said.

"First, I have obtained Mr. Cox's agreement not to have Newfield arrested immediately. Perhaps, if Cox has reason to believe that the money will eventually be repaid, he can be persuaded not to pursue his case against Newfield publicly."

"But how on earth could Victor possibly repay him?" Elizabeth asked.

"It would be a slow process, admittedly," Spencer replied. "But Newfield could begin repaying the loan with the proceeds of a job. That is at least some money—more money than Mr. Cox would obtain from him if he were in debtors' prison."

"Who in the world would hire Victor?" Elizabeth wondered.

"Yet again, the Oxford old boys' network has become a very useful tool." Spencer grinned, and Elizabeth's heart missed a beat or two. He was really most attractive when he smiled.

"Another former classmate of ours is Harry Saunderson," Spencer began.

"Oh, I remember him!" Benjamin exclaimed. "He came to Linden Park once at Christmas, did he not, because his family was abroad?"

"Yes, and his far-flung family is the very thing that shall save us now," Spencer replied. "Several weeks ago, I suspected that it might be necessary to find a place far from England where Victor could be quietly sent—'for his health,' perhaps.

"So I wrote to Harry to find out whether his family still owned a sugar plantation in Barbados. It turns out that they do, and they just happen to be in need of a steward."

Lord Langdon laughed. "Brilliant, Spence. So you will ship this Newfield off to the West Indies to act as the Saundersons' steward . . ."

". . . advising him that, if he decides to decline my generous offer—or, indeed, if any whisper of harm comes to Miss Scott in his absence—he may want to cancel his subscription to the *Evening Record-Gazette*." Finally, Spencer stopped moving and leaned against the blue-tiled fireplace surround, looking immensely pleased with himself.

He had reason to congratulate himself. It was a brilliant plan. Except . . .

"What if Victor decides to harm you when you deliver this proposition?" she cried. "I will not have that!"

A tiny smile flitted across his face before an expression of grim determination replaced it.

"I shall be careful," he said.

"Really, Mr. Willoughby, it is most unwise to put yourself in danger!" Aunt Harriet exclaimed.

"Yes, Spencer, there must be another way to carry this out, rather than confronting Mr. Newfield in person," said Lady Langdon.

"If we send a letter or an emissary, there is always the chance that Victor will simply go into hiding," Spencer said. "I think it best that I go in person. And I am glad to do it."

From her vantage point on one side of the room, Elizabeth spotted Benjamin looking at his younger brother with undisguised respect. Spencer missed the glance, however, as he was addressing Lord Langdon.

"Matt, would you mind if I borrowed your dueling pistols?"

"Dueling pistols?" Lady Langdon voice was sharp with distress. "Tell me, Matthew, we do not have such things in this house, do we?"

"Yes, my love, we do." Langdon rose from the settle and strolled across the room to a small Sheraton secretary. Opening a drawer, he removed some papers, lifted out what appeared to be a false bottom, and extracted a mahogany case. He closed the drawer, returned to the group gathered around the fire, and handed the case to Spencer.

"Didn't know you could shoot, Spence," he remarked with what Elizabeth suspected was studied indifference.

"Learned while you and the rest of the sporting men were flailing about on the football field at Oxford," Spencer said as he opened the case and withdrew an ivory-handled pistol. "Had to do something to occupy my time. I used to be quite good at it."

"Used to be?" Elizabeth heard that note of panic rising in her voice again.

"It is like reading—it is a skill that one does not easily

forget." His smile was brief. "I simply have not had much call to use it, until now."

"This is absolute madness . . ." Aunt Harriet began.

God bless her, Elizabeth thought. *Perhaps, if he won't listen to me, he will listen to her.*

But Spencer did not appear at all disposed to listen to any arguments against his plan.

"I doubt I shall have to use these, but it is wise to bring them, just in case," he was saying, ignoring Aunt Harriet's outburst.

"You shall need a second, Spence." Lord Langdon commented.

Elizabeth glanced at Lady Langdon to see her reaction to this proposal. Clarissa's face had gone pale and she had moved her hand from the settle to grip her husband's arm.

In the few hours since Elizabeth had arrived at Langdon Hall, she had already noticed the easy camaraderie and obvious affection the Langdons shared. But she knew, watching Lady Langdon's mobile face contract in a spasm of fear and anger, that they shared much more than that. To her shame, she was stabbed by a pang of pure, sharp jealousy for their loving, equal partnership.

She wondered whether her own face betrayed any of the same emotions as Lady Langdon's. Panicked in case Spencer, or anyone, should notice, she willed her mouth into a calm, firm line.

"Would you have me as your second, Spence?" Lord Langdon asked. Beside him, his wife took a deep breath.

"What, and take a newlywed man away from his honeymoon?" Spencer laughed. "What sort of mean-spirited scoundrel do I appear?"

"You are right, Spencer," drawled Benjamin, pushing off from the door frame against which he had been leaning. "It would be most unkind to choose a newly married man. I, however, have no such entanglements. I would be proud to serve as your second, should the need arise."

The two brothers exchanged an unreadable look. Spencer appeared to hesitate for a moment, then extended his hand to his brother.

"Thank you, Ben. I would be proud to have you."

The two men, so alike and yet so different, shook hands with a grave formality that made Elizabeth want to shout with frustration. And yet, she seemed to be unable to find her voice.

"Are you both deranged?" she finally managed to croak.

The regard of everyone in the room swiveled toward her.

"This is not a game!" she shouted, not caring who noticed the raw emotion in her voice. What would happen if Spencer or Ben was *killed?* This was no time for restraint on her part. "Victor is a determined man. He is large and he is violent."

"That, Miss Scott," said Spencer, as he turned toward the door, "is precisely why we must go."

Fifteen

Spencer gave Matthew's chestnut, Thunder, a gentle pat. "Don't worry, old boy. We shall stop soon for lunch, and you shall have a rest."

"What about you, Spencer?" Benjamin inquired from his seat on Apollo, another fine bit of blood from Matthew's stable. "Are you still in pain?" His voice was diffident.

"I am fine," Spencer lied, reluctant to tell his brother how his slowly healing shoulders flamed like fire beneath his blue riding coat. "But it will be most pleasant to break for a meal. I am famished."

"As am I—although, I admit, that is nothing new under the sun." Benjamin grinned.

Soon, the brothers reached a small inn at a tiny village called Creevy. Once settled in front of plates of thick lamb stew and two large tankards of ale, Spencer glanced at his brother. Seeing Benjamin focused on buttering a large slab of bread, he said casually, "I've a question for you, Ben."

"Yes?" Ben tore off a piece of bread, popped it into his mouth, and smiled.

"Have you ever considered offering for anyone?"

Benjamin swallowed. "A big oaf of a farmer like me?" He laughed. "Not really. The only time I even considered the idea was a few years ago, after one of those demmed *ton* balls you dragged me to. Remember Miss Nixon?"

Spencer hazily recalled a pretty, milk-and-water miss whom they had met shortly after she came out. If he remembered correctly, she had been rather popular with a group of young men who preferred women skilful at batting their eyelashes and at staying in the background.

"Yes, vaguely." He took a long draft of ale.

"I most enjoyed meeting her at first, and even took her out for a jaunt in Hyde Park."

"Really!" Spencer was amazed. He had no idea his shy sibling had done any such thing.

"But the odd thing was, that once we were ensconced in the carriage, we discovered we had very little to say to each other. It was truly the longest ride of my life!" Ben grinned at the memory and helped himself to another piece of bread.

"Talking—in carriages or out of them—has never been a problem for Miss Scott," Spencer said, remembering their last encounter in a moving conveyance, when she had so starkly refused his offer.

"Ah, yes, the intriguing Miss Scott." Ben's eyes lit up with mischief. "I suspected she was the subject of your matrimonial musings. So you are thinking of offering for her?"

"Not thinking. I already have." Spencer stared at his plate, his appetite waning as he recalled her curt refusal. He should not have been surprised.

His brother's eyes widened. "I take it the proposal was not a success."

"You could say that. She made it clear that it was unwelcome." He sketched out for his brother the details of the unfortunate incident.

"Are you mad?" Ben demanded when Spencer had finished.

"What do you mean?" Spencer felt a flicker of anger light up inside him. He should have known better than to expect understanding from Benjamin.

"I know very little about young ladies, but even I know enough to understand that they abhor being pursued for their money."

The flicker of anger burst into flame. "You think I offered for Miss Scott for her money?" he growled.

"Well, did you not? I know you are always short of funds for those experiments, and you just said that you told her that marrying you would be a perfect way to protect her funds."

"I could care less about her bloody fortune!" Spencer shouted, slamming his fork down on the rough wooden table. He ignored the startled looks cast their way by a group of older gentlemen seated near the hearth.

"Well, from what you've told me, she could not possibly know that from the ham-handed offer you made," Ben said mildly.

"She knows I am not a fortune hunter. I have told her I have all the funds I need. I was simply trying to persuade her that marrying me would be the best way to protect herself from Victor."

"Could you not think of a better reason for convincing her to marry you?"

"Well, I could have said I loved her—which I most assuredly do—but she would have laughed in my face," Spencer spat.

"I doubt that." Benjamin spooned up some lamb stew.

"Well, of course she would, Ben!" Spencer almost shouted, barely hiding his exasperation. "Here she is, probably one of the richest women in London. I am sure her house and its furnishings are far beyond anything I could ever provide. One has only to look at her garments to realize that she lives a life of quite lofty privilege."

"And?" Ben raised his eyebrows.

"And? And I am not in a similar position!" Spencer finally allowed his anger to show. "Even if the optics work succeeds, I shall never have that kind of wealth. I am just a fourth son, skilled at little and destined for less. I have no profession and no purpose in life, while she has both. What could I possibly offer her, aside from the opportunity to protect herself and her money from Newfield?"

"Again, I am no expert in this area, but it seems the one thing she cannot buy with all her wealth is companionship. You can offer her that." Ben gave his brother an encouraging smile.

"It is poor compensation." Spencer knew he was being mulish, but he did not care.

"Think what you will, Spence. But I have observed Miss Scott. I have seen her watching you when she thinks no one is looking. I have noticed her concern for you— even yesterday, when she was obviously angry with you. Now I know why she was angry," he added reflectively.

"So she watches me. That means nothing."

"It's the way she watches you, little brother. I may be wrong, but I would venture to say that the intensity of her regard has nothing to do with the fact that you saved her from Newfield." Benjamin grinned. "You spend too much time in that dim barn. It's destroying your eyesight."

"You spend too long outside in the hot sun, Ben," Spencer muttered, embarrassed. "It's destroying your mind." But inside him, the flame of anger went out, to be replaced by a faint, flickering glimmer of hope.

Spencer shifted his weight from foot to foot impatiently. It had been five minutes since a young clerk from Newfield and Son had scurried upstairs to look for Victor. The young man had appeared unnerved by Spencer's imperious command to summon the head of the company.

Spencer and his brother gazed about the establishment.

Oak shelves soared to the ceiling, and although most of them were half empty, the shop was filled with browsers. Every bit of glass and brass gleamed, and the counter was staffed by several poised, professional clerks.

"It does not look like the premises of a man on the way to debtors' prison," Ben murmured.

"It is astonishing what one can hide from prying eyes, if one wants to," Spencer replied. He noted, when looking at one of the shelves, that most of the bolts on it held only a small length of fabric. Glancing at adjacent shelves more closely, he realized that just about every bolt in the shop was a decoy.

Spencer willed his feet to keep still. He longed to pace. It helped him think.

It was another five minutes before Newfield deigned to appear. An ugly bruise purpled his chin, Spencer noted with unholy satisfaction. Newfield's eyes narrowed into slits when he realized the identity of his unexpected guests.

The clerk, clearly recognizing that expression, shot back behind the counter and loudly asked a perspiring, elderly customer if there was anything he could help her find.

"Willoughby." Victor's voice was like ice.

"Newfield." Spencer motioned to Ben. "My brother, Benjamin Willoughby."

Newfield gave an almost imperceptible nod, then shifted his irate gaze back to Spencer. "So, you have brought reinforcements this time."

"I seem to recall that I did not need reinforcements the last time we met."

A flush spread slowly across Newfield's face. "I believe this conversation would be more appropriately conducted in my office. Gentlemen?"

Newfield led the way up a staircase and along a dim

hallway into his office. Carelessly, he tossed a pile of papers off an old leather settee and gestured at his visitors.

"Have a seat. You'll forgive me if I don't offer you
tea and biscuits?" Newfield's mouth quirked into a garish
imitation of a smile.

"Certainly. We do not plan to stay long." Spencer
leaned toward him. "I must admit, I am surprised to see
you still on your premises, Newfield. I would have
thought you long fled in the face of your creditors."

Newfield's face flushed further. "I am working on
finding another source of funds to pay my debts. An old
friend in Bristol . . ."

Spencer cut him off. "What would you say if I offered
you the perfect way to escape public ruin?"

Newfield's mouth dropped open, revealing a set of yel-
lowed and unappealing teeth. "You? You want to repay
my debts?"

"Don't be mad, Newfield. I have neither the blunt nor
the desire to do any such thing." Spencer picked idly at
a piece of lint on his beige wool trousers.

"What, then? What magical solution do you propose?" Belligerence dripped from Victor's voice.

"How do you feel about a change of climate?"

"A what?"

"A change of climate. Perhaps the warm sun would
do your failing constitution some good."

"I don't have a failing constitution." Victor looked
away, and began noisily sifting through some papers.

"Are you certain? You appear to be bruising rather
easily these days." Spencer could not resist one small bit
of gloating.

His adversary looked up with a glower, but said nothing.

"I hear the West Indies have a very healthful climate,"
Ben remarked in a conversational tone.

"Do you?" Spencer tried to sound surprised.

"I have heard just the opposite," Newfield muttered. "Humidity, bugs, vicious winds, and appalling heat."

"But I understand the beaches are nice, if one cares for bathing." Spencer stretched his legs in front of him.

"Am I to assume there is eventually going to be some point to this conversation? Or should I just give you a sound thrashing now and be done with it? I think I have an old riding crop in one of these drawers." Newfield made a great show of rummaging through his battered oak desk.

Despite his efforts to maintain his self-control, Spencer felt a flash of anger at Newfield's reference to their earlier encounter. He willed himself to be calm, and to remember that he had a few trump cards to play.

"Do stop fidgeting, Newfield," he forced himself to drawl. "There is, as a matter of fact, a point. I have come here to offer you a position."

"I have a job, thank you. I have no need of your charity."

"Ah, but it isn't my charity. An old school friend of mine comes from a family with large holdings in Barbados. And it just so happens that they are in need of a steward for one of their sugar plantations."

Victor gave a short bark of laughter. "And you are suggesting *me*? I would not know one end of a farm from the other. I'm a City man, born and bred."

"You do know how to run an operation and how to supervise men. As long as there are no gaming tables in the vicinity, that is." Spencer made a great show of examining his fingernail.

Newfield erupted from behind the desk. "Now, look, Willoughby, my personal life is none of your . . ."

"Forgive me for interrupting, but I believe you have made it my business," Spencer interjected, standing as well. "By blackmailing and forcibly confining Miss Scott, you have brought your sordid affairs to my attention. And if you do not take the Saundersons up on their most generous job offer—which, I should point out, will also put you out of reach of your creditors—I shall make your recent activities more public knowledge."

"And how shall you do that?" Newfield's voice was scathing, but underneath the bluster Spencer detected a faint note of fear.

"Have you ever heard of the *Evening Record-Gazette?*"

Victor's face turned a deep and unbecoming red. He nodded.

"Well, it seems another old school friend of mine named John Davis is the proprietor of that very publication. And he is always looking for new bits of information to share with his readers. I don't believe he has run a good blackmail-and-kidnapping story in months."

"Not that I can recall," Benjamin chipped in with a sly smile.

"You would not do it! I do not believe this!" Newfield bellowed, his fear now unmistakable.

"I would, and you should."

Newfield pounded his fist on the desk. "I am to just leave England at your command—all because of what I did to that ape-leading second cousin of mine? This is preposterous! I would never have even considered marrying the baggage if I didn't so desperately need her money. I could certainly do better for myself than some blue blood's bastard."

Suddenly, the room went very still for Spencer. "What did you say?" he asked in a quiet voice.

"A bastard! That's what I said! That is how I have been blackmailing her all this time. She is not Roger Scott's daughter at all. Her mother was the doxy of Viscount Norchester. I overheard the entire story when I was a child, as my parents once discussed it. Elizabeth bloody Scott should not have that business. It should have been mine!" Victor's howl of long-harbored outrage shook the walls of the small office.

A bastard. Was that the secret that Elizabeth had been keeping to herself all this time? Was that why she thought they would not suit? Astonishment, confusion, and relief swept through Spencer simultaneously.

"You need not look so surprised," Victor growled. "Bloody baggage always did have ideas above herself. Stupid tart. No better than her mother."

Spencer advanced toward the desk, noting that the larger man did not flinch as he did so. "I should call you out for that remark."

"Elizabeth is no relative of yours. What reason have you to call me out?" Newfield's words were terse, but the color had begun to drain from his flushed face. Spencer noted his adversary's hand shaking as he fiddled with a carved wooden letter opener.

"I would like to make Elizabeth a relative of mine." Spencer's teeth ached from grinding them.

"Oh, I suspected as much. You want the silly chit for yourself. Not surprising—even Quality such as you are often short of ready cash."

"I mean it, Newfield. Choose a second." Spencer's heart pounded as he glared at his adversary.

Victor laughed, a sharp, unpleasant sound. "Stop pretending, Willoughby. You have neither the fortitude nor the skill for such a challenge."

"Do I not?" Spencer inquired in an indifferent tone. He reached into the traveling bag beside him and extracted the small mahogany case Matthew had given him. Clicking the hasp, he opened the case and displayed its contents to Newfield.

"I have tested these, Newfield. They are both in good working order." He paused, satisfied, as the final remnant of hue vanished from Victor's face. "So when and where shall we meet?" Now that he had made the decision to challenge Newfield, he felt a curious freedom. It was akin to the exhilaration he had felt when he clipped Newfield in the chin in St. Stephen the Martyr. This duel would settle the business once and for all.

Unless, of course, Victor did not have the courage to fight him on an equal footing.

"You are mad!" Newfield shouted. Spencer suspected Victor was attempting to make up in volume what he lacked in courage. A quick exchange of looks with his brother revealed that Benjamin felt the same.

"Dueling is illegal!" Newfield sputtered.

"So are kidnapping and extortion, I believe," Spencer commented, studying his fingernails again.

"Now see here, Willoughby . . ."

"No, you see here, Newfield. You have a choice. Either meet me tomorrow morning at a place of your choosing, or be ready to board the *Mary Louise*—a ship that is leaving Portsmouth next Monday for Bridgetown. It is that simple."

"And what if I choose a third option: to simply go into hiding until you get tired of this game and disappear back to your fine privileged life?" Victor cracked his knuckles, and eyed the Willoughbys with an insolent glare.

"That could be rather difficult. You see, I have taken the liberty of approaching some . . . friends . . . of yours. A few of your creditors. It appears that at least one of them has been recovering from a dreadful assault for the last several weeks."

Victor gaped.

"Yes, he said that he suspected a man to whom he had lent money had set two thugs upon him to convince him not to get an arrest warrant."

Newfield's mouth flapped open and closed like that of a dying fish, but no sound emerged.

"I have intimated to Mr. Cox that you might agree to

pay back at least part of your loan if he refrained from speaking to the sheriff immediately."

Victor smacked the wall beside him with the flat of his hand. "So it is Cox you spoke to! Well, I have bested you on that score. Cox has absolved me of my loan. I have only some smaller creditors to worry about now."

"Do you have a letter outlining Cox's promise?" Spencer asked.

Victor shook his head.

"Did he tell you himself?"

Slowly, realization began to dawn in Newfield's dull eyes. Again, he shook his head.

"Then, once again, you are without proof of someone else's promise. Really, Newfield, you have to start getting these things in writing." Spencer chuckled as he willed himself to remain calm. If there was ever a situation where insouciance was called for, this was it. "It looks to me as though, in the eyes of the law, you are still required to pay back your debt to Mr. Cox."

Newfield spluttered, "Pay it back? With what? I used the last ready blunt I had to purchase that blasted special license!"

Spencer cast the corners of his mouth down in mock distress. "I am most sorry to hear that, Newfield. I believe that Mr. Cox is planning to ask the sheriff for an arrest warrant this afternoon. Unless, of course, you let him know within the next few hours that you plan to pay off your debt to him in stages—with your earnings from your new job in the West Indies."

Newfield balled one huge hand into a fist. With his other hand, he picked up the letter opener he had discarded on the desk.

"Do you think"—Spencer turned to his brother—"that John Davis would be interested in adding assault and coercion to the tales of kidnapping and blackmail already attached to Mr. Newfield? Oh, and don't forget utter cowardice in the face of a challenge. And, of course, the trial that will likely ensue if Mr. Cox discovers that Mr. Newfield is unable to pay his debts."

"I believe that information would interest Davis greatly," Benjamin replied, a gleam of admiration in his eye. "With these extra tidbits, he could serialize the article over several days. Sell more newspapers."

"All right!" Victor roared, throwing the letter opener back down on the desk. "You win."

Spencer blinked. "I beg your pardon?"

"You win! I shall take your demmed position and go off to the godforsaken West Indies. You can escort me to Portsmouth yourself." Victor sighed, and the act seemed almost to shrink him. He fell back against his battered chair. "I am heartily sick of running and hiding. If to live free, I must live in Barbados, so be it."

"There are two more things I must insist on before recommending you to the Saundersons," Spencer said, controlling his exultation over Victor's capitulation.

"What are they?" Newfield muttered, his voice devoid of emotion.

"One, you must continue to repay all your creditors—not just Mr. Cox—from your steward's wages."

Victor sputtered, "But that could take years!"

"You should have thought of that before you sat down at the gaming tables."

Newfield glowered, then gave a curt nod.

"And two, you must promise that no harm shall come to Miss Scott in your absence."

"How exactly am I to harm the bloody baggage if I am half a world away?" A hint of Victor's characteristic sneer crept back into his face.

"You appear to have several minions willing to do your bidding. Reynolds and Roberts, for two."

"And what shall you do if I refuse to comply?"

"I am assuming that you will eventually return to England, once your debts are repaid."

Victor nodded.

"Although I don't imagine you will be taking up the reins at Newfield and Son again."

Newfield groaned. "Not likely. The building, and everything in it, is mortgaged to the hilt. The moment I disappear, it will all likely be sold."

"But you should like to get back into the drapery business, I assume?"

"It would be one possibility."

"Well, then. Promise me that no harm shall come to Elizabeth, and I shall do my best to keep the reasons for your disappearance from England a secret. I shall talk to my friend at the *Evening Record-Gazette*. Perhaps he can be prevailed upon to write a piece about your failing health and the restorative effects of tropical breezes.

"I cannot promise anything on that score," Spencer added. "But I can promise you this. If I ever hear one word of even a rumor of a threat to Miss Scott—either a threat to her person, or a hint of a rumor about her parentage—I will spread the news of your illegal doings to every newspaper and gossip in London, and beyond. I believe that would make it quite impossible for you to ever reenter business in England again."

Newfield hung his head, the picture of defeat. "All right, Willoughby. All right. Your precious Miss Scott shall remain unharmed. It is no great sacrifice on my part, anyway," he added, with a trace of his old bluster. "The chit is useless to me now. And, if she has managed to wrap up her blunt as she says she has, she will be most useless to you as well. It really was the only thing that saved her from being a complete antidote."

Spencer rose from his chair, rage coursing through him at Newfield's remarks, halting only when he felt Benjamin's restraining hand on his arm.

"Spence, we have Mr. Newfield's agreement. I think it is time we took him home to help him pack for his journey. Do you not agree?"

With an effort, Spencer relaxed and nodded. He had no need of violence anymore. He had won this battle with words.

Sixteen

"So we are finished, Mr. Mason?" Elizabeth made to rise from her chair.

"We are finished, Miss Scott." The portly solicitor rose from behind the desk in Lord Langdon's cozy office and extended his hand to her. Then, as if realizing that shaking hands was not the protocol for concluding a business arrangement with a young woman, he awkwardly withdrew it and stuck it into the pocket of his worn morning coat.

Elizabeth, well used to the discomfort men seemed to experience in her presence, merely smiled. "Thank you again for all your hard work on my behalf, sir. I truly appreciate it. I know that it has been particularly inconvenient because it has required you to travel several times, to different places."

"That is no matter, Miss Scott," he replied, returning to the desk to gather together the many sheets she had just signed and sanded. Blowing the remaining grit off each one, he replaced them in his traveling case. "It was my pleasure." He flashed her a tentative smile, an effort that seemed to pain him. Elizabeth suspected his smiles were rather weak and rusty due to lack of use.

The young footman standing at the door escorted Mr. Mason to the foyer, leaving Elizabeth alone with her thoughts in the charming study.

So she was now free to return to London. She could leave today if she so desired. But did she so desire?

Spencer was still in London, and no word had arrived as to his success—or lack thereof—in convincing Victor to flee to the West Indies. Elizabeth shivered, despite the glowing fire in the hearth nearby. If he had succeeded quickly, he might return today. But if things had not gone as planned . . .

She refused to dwell on what might have happened. Such thoughts had kept her largely sleepless since the day Spencer and his brother had left for London. What if Spencer challenged Victor to a duel? And what if Spencer lost? She would never be able to live with herself.

She told herself she should not care so deeply. Yes, it would be tragic if Spencer Willoughby lost his life on her account. But she had tried to talk him out of his folly. They all had. She could not hold herself to blame if he came to a bad end, she reasoned, using the objective, critical faculties her father had trained her to develop.

But objectivity was failing her in this case. If something happened to Spencer, she would not be able to live with herself because—despite his clumsy, cold offer, despite everything—she loved him.

Could he possibly be risking his well-being at Victor's hands because he loved her? The thought crossed her mind for at least the one-hundredth time. And for at least the one-hundredth time she posed a question in return. If he loved her, why then did he not say so in the carriage when he made his offer?

Around and around her thoughts progressed, following the same rutted track they had been stuck in for days.

It did not matter whether he loved her or not. As a man's unacknowledged by-blow, she was no fit match for Spencer Willoughby.

Desperate to distract herself, and unwilling to rejoin

the Langdons or her aunts until she had had time to digest the fact that her legal problems were resolved, she glanced around the masculine study.

The furniture was upholstered in a rich green velvet, and the walls paneled in glowing cherry wood. Over the fireplace hung a portrait of a young couple whom she assumed to be Lord Langdon's parents. Dressed in the fashions of her own parents' youth, they were both smiling widely for the artist. The young man had his hand protectively around his wife's waist and was gazing at her with unconcealed affection. She, for her part, had leaned toward him in a most charming manner.

A love match, obviously.

"It is a captivating painting, is it not?" Lord Langdon's voice from the doorway startled her.

"Yes, my lord." She rose from her chair.

"Please, Miss Scott, do not stand on ceremony here. You are my guest. Please simply call me Matthew—or Langdon, if you prefer."

Elizabeth did not think she could manage either with this kind but rather imposing man. Unlike his friend Spencer, he did not seem to be a man used to great informality. So she simply nodded and said, "Thank you for your kindness."

He acknowledged her gratitude with a nod and strolled into the room. "My eye is always drawn to that portrait when I am working here," he commented, as he stood before the fire. "They were so happy together."

"They are your parents, I assume?"

"My aunt and uncle, actually. They raised me after my parents were killed in a carriage accident, when I was a child."

Perhaps that tragedy explained part of the air of reserve Lord Langdon carried around with him. She sensed he would not appreciate an expression of sympathy, however, so she merely nodded.

"My aunt is deceased. My Uncle Walter lives with me in London. He is quite ill, and I felt terrible leaving him in the care of servants, but he insisted that Clarissa and I take several weeks to ourselves after our wedding. He was so adamant about it that I thought it would do his health more good for us to leave than to stay." He smiled ruefully, as he sat down behind the desk Mr. Mason had recently vacated. "Uncle Walter has always been very good at getting what he wants in the end. He was one of the people who encouraged me to make a love match myself, instead of the business arrangement I originally desired."

"You and Lady Langdon certainly seem most happy together."

His smile widened. "That we are, although we almost were not married at all."

"Really?" Despite her own worries, Elizabeth was intrigued. Lord Langdon did not seem to be a man for whom things did not work out exactly as he had planned them.

"It is a long and convoluted story. But Spence played a big part in it, especially at the beginning. After an inauspicious first meeting, Clarissa and I likely would never have spoken to each other again if it had not been for Spence. He convinced us to get to know each other a bit better." Lord Langdon chuckled. "The man is an incurable romantic."

"Indeed." Elizabeth reflected that she had seen little evidence of this sentimental streak.

"Miss Scott . . ." her host began.

"Please, call me Elizabeth," she interrupted.

"Thank you, I shall." He paused. "Elizabeth, I know it is not my place to interfere, and you must believe me when I say that I am usually the last person to become entangled in other people's personal business."

She nodded warily.

"I have known Spence since we were young, and I truly believe him to be one of the most honorable, steadfast men of my acquaintance. But I cannot help suspecting that you do not share this view."

"Mr. Willoughby has been more than kind to me and my family," she said carefully, wondering where on earth this conversation was leading. "I shall never be able to repay his efforts."

"But do you respect him?" Lord Langdon's voice took on a strange urgency.

"Of course," she said with surprise.

"So many people do not, you know. They take one look at him, and his seeming lack of occupation, and dismiss him as a fribble. Even his own family does so."

"I have noticed that," she replied. "I am at a loss to understand it, however. It appears that they have done everything they can to discourage him from pursuing a suitable profession, and that they do not understand his optics work. I do not mean to disparage them, of course, for they were so hospitable to me . . ."

"Of course, Elizabeth, I understand." Lord Langdon cut her off. "But your observations are completely correct. And his family's disapproval has always made Spence a bit less than confident."

"Spencer lacking in confidence?" In her astonishment, she used his Christian name. "He is the soul of confidence. Look at the way he convinced us all to let him hare off to London. The man should have been a diplomat. He can easily take control of a room and hold all and sundry captivated to his latest plot, no matter how disparaging everyone is." Realizing she might have revealed a bit too much of her admiration for Mr. Willoughby, she stopped.

Lord Langdon gave her a shrewd glance. Too late, she remembered that he was a particularly active member of the House of Lords, well used to reading people.

He stood up and walked around the desk, then took the wing chair next to hers.

"So you also recognize Spence's qualities?" he murmured.

"Yes." There was no use denying it.

"Then, may I ask, why is there such a coldness between you?"

"You may ask, my . . . Langdon," she replied. "But I would prefer not to discuss it."

"As you wish." He nodded. "I understand your desire for privacy, as it is one I share. Do know, however, that Spence admires you in return."

Her head shot up, and a small seedling of hope germinated inside her.

"As I said, I have known Spence for many years. We have been through many interesting times together, particularly in the years after we first came down from Oxford." He grinned—actually grinned!

Grinning herself, Elizabeth could well imagine what those interesting times entailed. A great deal of brandy and some pretty actresses, if she had her guess.

"I have seen Spence interested in many women, and pursued by many others. But I have never seen him look at any female the way he regarded you the other day, as he left for London."

Resolutely quashing the hope that was growing inside her, she replied, "That may be, but the fact remains that he and I come from two different spheres. Now that my affairs are in order, I must return to London. My business . . ."

". . . shall continue to run without you for a few more days," Lord Langdon interjected. "You do not plan to leave immediately?"

"No. I shall wait until Mr. Willoughby returns." *If he returns,* she added silently.

Her face must have registered some of her fear, because Lord Langdon reached across the small space between them and awkwardly patted her hand in a brotherly gesture. "Do not worry, Elizabeth. Spence is not one to take foolhardy risks. He will return shortly. I am certain of it."

"I know," she replied in a strangled voice.

He gave her a sympathetic look and rose. "I must attend to some matters in the stables," he said. "But do consider what I have said. I believe I know Spence almost as well as he knows himself. And I believe that he cares for you more than you realize."

With that, he quit the room, leaving Elizabeth alone with her repetitious thoughts.

If he cared for her so much, why did he not say so?

Furious with herself for mooning about the house like a green girl, she stood up and shook out her creased skirts. She had been sitting for what seemed like hours, first discussing the final legal papers with Mr. Mason, then engaging in that odd discussion with Lord Langdon. What she really needed was a long, long walk. It would clear her head.

Spencer approached the drive to Langdon Hall with some trepidation. He had good news for Elizabeth, of course. But would she remain long enough at Matthew's home to celebrate?

His uncertainty about her willingness to remain once her affairs were in order had spurred him to return to the country immediately. He had left to Benjamin the distasteful task of escorting Newfield to Portsmouth.

"Do not worry about me, Spencer," his brother had said. "I can handle one lout on my own. Go back to Langdon's place and repair things with Miss Scott."

With some guilt, he had accepted Ben's offer and returned at top speed to Oxfordshire. But now that he had arrived, he found himself uncharacteristically nervous about encountering Elizabeth. What if Ben had been wrong? What if she cared nothing for him? The embarrassment of listening to her refuse him a second time would be almost unbearable.

Buck up, he admonished himself. *If you could stare down Newfield's gun barrel, you can certainly face whatever a small, unarmed woman can toss at you.*

He grinned weakly.

Rounding a bend in the long drive up to Matt's estate, he saw a lone figure walking toward him on the far verge. A petite figure whose long blue skirt was whipping about in the light breeze.

Elizabeth.

His heart contracted at the sight of her. He had to make her understand that he loved her. And he had to hope against hope that that would be enough.

Urging Matt's roan into a gallop, he thundered along the road until he was within speaking distance of Elizabeth. She glanced behind her, as if weighing her options for escape. They were not within sight of the house, any of its outbuildings, or any of the estate's employees.

There was nowhere she could turn. She would have to hear him out.

Reining in his horse, he trotted to the spot where she had stopped. He leaped down lightly and gave the horse's flank a gentle pat. The horse wisely ambled off to the shade of a nearby oak.

"Good day, Miss Scott." He drank in the sight of her. Her cheeks, flushed by the wind, were pink and glowing. The wind had also torn loose a few chestnut curls, which dangled most appealingly from beneath her simple yellow bonnet.

Impulsively, uncertain how his action would be received, he raised her gloved hand to his lips and kissed it. To his delight, she neither grimaced nor pulled away.

"Welcome back, Mr. Willoughby," she replied, gazing at him with a most odd expression. To his astonishment, she squeezed his hand gently before withdrawing her own. "It is so very, very good to see you safe and well. I was most concerned for your welfare in London."

He should have regretted making her worry, but he did not. Her regard gave him the inspiration he needed to say what he had resolved to say.

Before he could begin, however, she glanced behind him. "But where is your brother? I hope he is also unharmed?" She frowned and gripped his arm.

Ignoring the warmth her touch engendered in him, he forced himself to pat her hand in a most platonic fashion. "Ben is completely well. In fact, at this moment, he and Newfield are likely on their way to Portsmouth. Victor is due to leave England shortly for a new and fascinating career as a plantation steward." Spencer permitted himself a grin of triumph.

"Oh, Mr. Willoughby, what glorious, glorious news!" Elizabeth cried, casting her arms about his neck and giving him an impulsive hug.

It was all he could do not to kiss her soundly right there, in the middle of the Langdon Hall park. She was so soft and warm against him. He laid his cheek atop her head and breathed in her heady scent, a mixture of rosewater and some indefinable perfume that was most uniquely hers.

Knowing it was wrong, but unable to stop, he wrapped his arms around her small waist and pulled her more tightly to him. Not for the first time, he marveled at her soft curves. With her roundness pressed against his chest, he was unable to think about much else.

They stayed that way for a moment or two, and then Spencer released his grip. Elizabeth, as if realizing the inappropriateness of their embrace, unlaced her hands from around his neck, and stepped away. Embarrassment stained her cheeks an even brighter pink.

"Forgive me," she murmured. "I should not have done that."

"I cannot say that I am sorry that you did."

They stood in silence for a moment. Desperate to break the odd tension in the air, Spencer asked, "Shall I tell you how Ben and I convinced Newfield to adhere to our plan?"

"Yes, please. I am most anxious to hear all the details."

Quickly, he related the story of the encounter in Newfield's office, leaving out the part of the conversation that had dealt with Elizabeth's parentage. He wanted to let her tell him in her own fashion, if she was so inclined.

At the end of the tale, she laughed until tears trickled down her cheeks. "Oh, I would so have loved to have seen it! Did I not tell you that Victor is, at heart, a coward? I must admit, however, that I am glad you were not involved in a duel with him. I would never have forgiven myself if anything had happened to you on my account."

He smiled, then an awkward silence once again settled over them.

He would never get a better opportunity to say what he had imagined saying during the long journey from London.

"I know I made a dreadful hash of this the last time, Elizabeth, but I must try again." Spencer inhaled a deep draft of fresh country air. "Would you do me the greatest honor, and consent to be my wife?"

She screwed up her face into such a contortion he felt certain she was about to cry.

"But why, Spencer?" she asked, raising her face to his. He saw that her eyes were indeed bright with unshed tears. "Victor is no longer a threat. You no longer need to shield me."

"I know that." He smiled at her. "I still want to marry you."

"Then why?"

Because I love you, you silly chit, he longed to say. He hesitated. It was a poor reason, but it was the truth. Would it be enough?

As he paused, trying to find the right words, her face took on a most displeased expression.

"If you still feel some misguided responsibility to protect me, you need not bother," she said, each word piercing his brain like a sharp icicle. "Mr. Mason has departed not an hour ago, with all the signed papers needed to safeguard my inheritance. It is now completely safe, as am I."

The tension that had been building inside him over the miles from London suddenly erupted.

"I do not care about your blasted fortune!" he shouted.

She stepped back from him, her expression wary.

"Do you truly think I wanted to marry you only to protect your money?"

She nodded, nibbling on her lower lip.

"I want you, dammit. You! But since you obviously think me not good enough for you, just say so. Stop hiding behind your bloody money." With that admission, his fury was spent, as quickly as it had come. He felt exhausted.

"When did I ever give you the impression that I thought you were not good enough for me?" Elizabeth's voice was subdued.

"Elizabeth, I am not blind, nor ignorant in the ways of the world." It hurt to bring his most private fears out for her derision, but he had to make her understand. "I am a fourth son, with a meager income, no property, and few prospects. The estates will all go to my oldest brother when my father passes on. I have no profession, no purpose in life. You have always lived in wealth, a wealth that I suspect exceeds my family's own. I could not keep you in such estate. You could make a far more brilliant match than an alliance with me."

"I care nothing for any man's wealth," she retorted with some heat. "I am more than comfortable for the rest of my life. My needs are small, truly.

"But more to the point, I would not say you have no prospects," she added. He glanced at her, surprised. "Why must you believe what others say, just because they have been saying it all your life?"

"What are you talking of?"

"You are convinced you have nothing to offer the world, because your family has told you so. I have seen the way they dismiss you, and it makes me angry. But you have so much to offer. It is not every man who could have saved me from Victor." She smiled. "And it is not every man who could conduct such experiments as you are conducting."

"No one believes in those experiments—no one save myself and my investor."

"I believe." Elizabeth's eyes were shining as she raised her face to his. "I know you shall succeed. You are intelligent and courageous and intrepid and all the other things one needs to be to advance the cause of knowledge. Do not care a whit about what others think. *I* believe."

Touched beyond words by the strength of her conviction, he acted rather than spoke. Grasping her by the waist, he swung her around until she laughed like a child, and her bonnet tumbled off her head.

When he placed her feet back on the ground, she leaned against him dizzily.

"Spencer, whatever were you thinking?" she asked with a shaky laugh.

It was his name on her lips that undid him. To hell with the consequences, he thought.

"I love you, Elizabeth," he murmured. Lord, it felt so good to say it at last.

She did not laugh. "I love you too," she replied, her eyes confirming what her lips had said.

He gathered her into his arms, bent his head toward her, and kissed her.

She tasted just as sweet as he had remembered. And she was as responsive as she had been that evening in the Linden Park kitchen. Her lips parted beneath his, inviting him to deepen the kiss.

Elizabeth almost gasped as Spencer responded to her unconscious invitation. She knew they must stop, that this marriage could not happen. He would not want her, once he knew the truth of her birth.

But his kiss was robbing her of the ability to think of anything further in the future than the next five minutes.

Impulsivity had been her downfall her entire life. Why should today be any different? she thought, as she relaxed and gave herself up to Spencer's caress. Tomorrow would be soon enough to go back to her own life.

Spencer had moved away from her lips and was gently kissing the rest of her face: gentle yet insistent kisses on her cheeks, her forehead, even her eyelids. She heard herself sigh, and did not care.

The rough stubble of his unshaven chin grazed her throat as he nibbled on her earlobe. She shuddered with pleasure as tingles of excitement radiated throughout her body.

"Do you have even the faintest idea what you do to me, Elizabeth?" he whispered in her ear.

"I believe I am beginning to understand," she murmured back. "I may need some more clues, though."

With a low moan that she felt rather than heard, he skimmed his hands over her shoulders and down the lace that framed her throat. As though she could not help herself, she arched toward him. Her body was tingling. She had never felt more gloriously alive. . . .

"God, Elizabeth, we must stop." Almost roughly, he pushed himself away from her. "If we do not stop now, we shall not stop at all. And much as I would enjoy that"—he laughed raggedly—"it would not be wise. Not unless, that is, you have reconsidered my offer?"

His question brought Elizabeth back to reality with a sickening thud. "Spencer, nothing would give me more joy than to accept it."

He grinned.

"But . . ."

The grin faded.

"I am not a fit wife for you." Good heavens, how was she to explain?

"I think you are more than fit." He favored her with his most rakish grin.

Why did I let him kiss me? she cried silently. It was just making this so much more difficult.

Backing up a little, she pointed to a disused stile a short distance across a field. "Would you mind if we sat down?"

"Not at all," he replied.

They walked in silence to the stile. In her heightened state of awareness, she seemed to notice every lark's song, every folded hill in the distance, each blade of new grass, the fresh smell of early roses in the air. How could she feel so alive, when her dream was about to die?

Once settled upon the stile, she turned to face him. She could barely speak for the sadness that engulfed her.

"I am not entirely the woman you believe me to be," she began.

"You are not the love of my life?" he replied, resting his hand gently upon her leg. Just as gently, she removed it.

"I had believed all my life that Roger Scott was my

father," she said. "But when my mother was ill, earlier this year, she told me that that was not true."

Spencer nodded but did not speak. He did not seem shocked, but she could not tell. His face was devoid of expression.

Recklessly, she plunged ahead. "You see, my father often traveled abroad when we were young. He had sailed to Jamaica to meet with some of the planters there when my brother, Tony, was just a toddler. He was due to return for Christmas. But three weeks before Christmas, my mother received word that his ship, the *Intrepid*, had been lost in the waters off the Bahamas. All aboard were presumed drowned.

"She refused to believe the news at first. But as the months wore on and no word arrived from my father—I mean, her husband—she eventually accepted that he had died.

"For many months, she was inconsolable. But then, one day, she went to visit a friend of hers who had married a young baron. The friend's husband arrived home with a group of his acquaintances in tow. One of those acquaintances was a man named Viscount Norchester."

Spencer took her hand. She knew she should withdraw it, but she needed the support he offered.

"I shall not bore you with the details. Let it just be said that this Norchester seduced my mother. I do not blame her," she added with spirit. "She was young, and lonely, and heartbroken. She also believed that Norchester wanted to marry her.

"But when he learned she was *enceinte*"—she felt herself blushing at the frank nature of this discussion, but she forced herself to continue—"he dismissed her entirely and refused to acknowledge the child she carried. I am that child."

Spencer nodded. To Elizabeth's amazement, his grasp on her hand tightened.

"When my mother was three months along, my father suddenly returned to England. His ship had indeed capsized, but he and several other passengers had been rescued by a passing fishing boat. They were taken to a small island, where several of them, including my father, immediately developed some sort of fever. He was unconscious for several weeks, and too weak to travel for months more. He attempted several times to get word to my mother of his whereabouts, but none of the letters had arrived.

"My father—Roger Scott, I mean—was a good man. He loved my mother, and he understood how she had come to act the way she had. He acknowledged me as his, and always treated me as Tony's equal in every way." She sighed. The stabbing pain of her parents' loss had diminished somewhat in the months since their passing, but she suspected it would be many years, if ever, before it completely disappeared.

"So you see, Spencer, I am not a fit match for anyone of your station. Not only am I a cit, I am not even legitimate."

Finally, she dared look up to see how her revelation had affected Spencer. She expected to see disgust or revulsion writ across his fine features. What she saw instead was a huge grin.

"Do you think this is a joke?" she demanded.

"No, my love, I do not," he replied. "I believe it to be true because you say it is. I also know it to be true because Newfield told me."

"Victor told you?" She gasped.

"Yes. He seemed to think I would care." He continued to grin. "Goodness, Elizabeth, if that is all that is troubling you, do not give it another thought."

"But it is a scandal! If word of it got out in the City . . ."

". . . yes, perhaps among the good merchants of the

City, such a revelation would be devastating. I can only imagine how much more above reproach you must need to be, as a woman in a man's world."

She nodded, overcome with emotion. No one, not even her aunts, had ever understood how difficult it was to be a female running a business.

"But my world is a different place, as you keep reminding me."

"I do not understand."

"Elizabeth, half the people I know are the products of liaisons between partners who were not married to each other."

She blinked in astonishment.

"Many marriages among the so-called upper classes are arranged, and more often than not the arrangements are not particularly congenial." He laughed. "Once the wife in such a marriage has produced an heir, the partners often tacitly agree to pursue other, shall we say, interests."

"I had no idea." Elizabeth breathed faintly. Could this really be true? Could it be her salvation?

"You need look no further than the Prince Regent and his errant consort to see that this is so. Do you not read the gossip columns?" he asked.

"Rarely. I am usually too busy reading the shipping reports to bother much with news of the aristocracy." Despite herself, a trace of what she had once thought was unshakeable disdain for the upper classes crept into her voice.

"Ah, but now I understand where your dislike of 'the Quality' comes from," Spencer said, as if reading her thoughts. "What Norchester—whom I do not know, by the way—did to you and your family was utterly despicable. But not all aristocrats are like him. Most work hard on their estates, work hard for their tenants. Or work on other projects," he added, in an apparent afterthought.

"I know that," she mumbled humbly. "Now."

Spencer smiled as he took her other trembling hand in his. "So you believe that not all aristocrats are indolent louts?" he inquired.

"Not all," she answered with a sly grin.

"And you believe me when I say that it matters not to me whether your father was Roger Scott, or a debauched viscount . . . or a London street sweeper?"

She nodded.

He wagged a finger at her with mock sternness. "Is there any other reason that I should not ask my question once again?"

Elizabeth tilted her head to one side and pretended to think. Then something actually did occur to her.

"Would you be adverse to the idea of my continuing to have a hand in the firm?" she asked, suddenly serious. "I do enjoy it so."

"You can stand on your head in the middle of Cavendish Square in a rainstorm for all that it matters to me, Elizabeth!" he roared. "I would not want to change one thing about you, and the company is part of who you are."

Love so strong it nearly took her breath away flooded through Elizabeth, mixed with relief and a heady, sweet joy.

"All right, then. I am getting weary of repeating this, so I will do it just one last time." Spencer laughed, then squeezed both of her hands inside his larger, warmer ones. "Miss Elizabeth Scott—fully legally protected heiress, London business magnate, and unacknowledged offspring of Viscount Norchester—will you *please* do me the honor of becoming my bride?"

"Yes!" Elizabeth shouted, withdrawing her hands so she could fling her arms around his neck. "Yes, yes, yes!"

ABOUT THE AUTHOR

Laura Paquet lives with her husband and three insane cats in Ottawa, Canada. *Miss Scott Meets Her Match* is her second Regency romance. She would love to hear from her readers. Please write to her at Box 215, 372 Rideau Street, Ottawa, Ontario, Canada K1N 1G7, or send her an e-mail at laura@cornerstoneword.com. And please visit her Web site at www.Laura ByrnePaquet.com for news of signings and upcoming books.

More Zebra Regency Romances